THE
ARK

J SWIFT

Cover designed by MiblArt

ISBN: 978-1-7398018-0-9

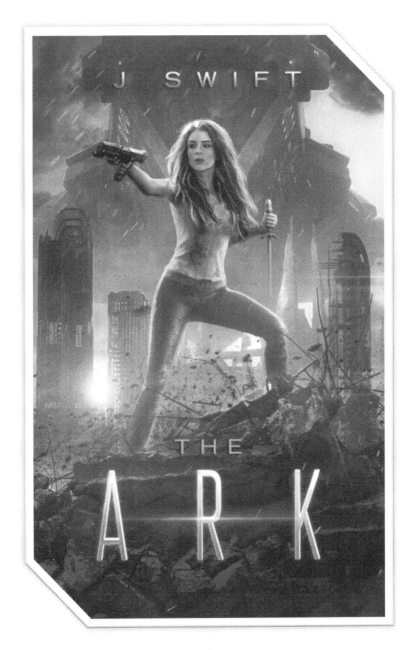

For Ken
Thanks for all the coffee

PROLOGUE

NEW AMERLAND WAS DESIGNED AND BUILT BY survivors of the Incident.

Those were the people who by some miracle managed to get underground before the bombs fell; managed to lock away themselves and their families, and to survive the worst nuclear attack in history.

Underground bunkers holding thousands were spread across the country. Some people were rich enough to have their own. Designed by the host cities, they were not glamorous – but they did the job they were designed to do and protected their residents from a brutish existence and early death.

For a decade the people were trapped. Unable to go topside and with no way of communicating with others, it was easy to understand why some of them lost their senses, and their sense of morality. There were horror stories of the inhabitants of little communal bunkers going deranged and turning cannibal. Tunnelling their way into other communities and decimating the survivors there. There was no way to warn others, and the groups moved undetected from place to place.

Eventually people started carving their way out of their bunkers. One shelter met with another and became stronger by numbers. Then they moved on and found others. Over the years huge facilities were designed and created, reinforced against attack. In time they moved upwards, back to the surface of the planet – and with that move came over-ground accommodation. Each city had a Complex. Some were designed with beauty and aesthetics in mind, intricate and rich, with indoor parks, academies and art galleries.

Silver City was planned by some of the greatest artists of the day. They filled it with bubble parks and exquisite buildings. It was the city for the rich. New Amerland was smaller, filthier and much less well endowed. While Silver City rose from what used to be open fields, when the residents of New Amerland broke through they were faced with the difficult task of building a complex within the confines of what used to be a city filled with skyscrapers and apartment buildings – towering blocks of brick and mortar, the skeletons of which survived the attack and imposed upon the builders the constraints of their existence.

Nevertheless, a complex was created and a board of governors was elected. In time, the scientists announced the inauguration of Project Ark, charged with saving humanity from a burning and wasted planet.

It had seemed that the inevitable fate of humankind was that those who survived one thing would be challenged by another. But the human race was strong: the battle for survival would be fought and won.

A site was required for development and manufacturing operations, and New Amerland was selected. The Arks would be monstrous, shapeless entities that would be capable of carrying fifty thousand crew and passengers. One would be launched every two years, reaching into the galaxy to colonise the fabled New World.

The rich would buy their tickets and travel as cosseted and privileged passengers. Those who did were afforded a luxurious experience, with first class rooms and facilities that put even Silver City to shame.

A lucky few would be selected by lottery and handed a ticket for free – but the chances were slim. Most people worked towards the aptitude test, for which every citizen was eligible at twenty-five. If they passed with a high score they were automatically given a place. With a low score their credentials were considered. Failure meant remaining on Earth for life. As sad as it was, at least fifty percent failed the test, and were fated to die on their desolate and degraded planet...

CHAPTER ONE

THE SUNLIGHT GAVE HIS SANDY HAIR A GOLDEN halo. Sitting on the short grass beside his father, Louis Andover sighed deeply and looked up at the synthetic sky. The colour was a beautiful deep blue, gently dotted with little puffs of white. He might have called the scene poetic. Instead, it was just peaceful. It was their little hideaway. A place they could go to get away from the realities of life. They were surrounded by daisies and cowslips. Louis always wanted to make little chains but at the back of his mind was the thought that it seemed like a girly thing to do. They did love the outdoors though. Even if it wasn't real, the holograms were so amazingly detailed you'd never know. You could even smell the flowers. It wasn't cheap of course. A day in the HoloChambers could cost up to a thousand credits. But to father and son sitting together it was priceless. They could afford it, of course – as a captain, Clarke Andover was a rich man. But should it cost a million credits they would still pay it. Just to enjoy the silence.

'TIME'S UP FOLKS! MOVE ON OUT!' The voice was deep and rough and cut through their quiet like a knife. Every time, it ended this way and every time it caught them off-guard. As they got to their feet Louis looked at his father.

'Dad?'

'Yes Louis?' His father's voice was almost a deeper version of his own. They both had the hint of a southern accent.

'We're not gonna be coming here for much longer, are we.' Louis looked at his feet. It was more of a statement than a question.

'No son, we're not. But we will find a place like this; one that we can stay in for days if we want. One that's really outside. We can go camping!'

Louis chuckled at the thought of his father sleeping in a tent. Clarke looked down at his son and grinned. 'What's so funny about that, huh?' He laughed along with his son.

They made their way through the trees and foliage. It really was a beautiful garden; whoever designed it was truly a poet. They moved between purple ferns and tall red trees. The flowers came in fantastic shades of pink and blue. Bright yellow and orange butterflies floated through the air around them, making the garden come alive. They walked alongside a little river that rushed down a gentle slope. There were beautiful birds in iridescent colours poking their beaks into the water. Louis watched as he walked; his father's hand was on his shoulder, guiding him in the right direction.

They reached the door and looked at the burly doorman. His shirt had ridden up his stomach revealing a pasty white, hairy belly. The smell was awful. He was wearing navy overalls with patches of sweat under his arms. He looked bored and sounded it too.

'Thank you for choosing Smithson's Holo-Chambers for all your holographic needs. Would you like to book your next visit now?'

'No thank you my friend. Have a good today.'

'You too Sir.' He turned to the control panel and hit a few buttons. The garden melted away and was replaced with a green room.

Louis walked down the metallic hall with his father without
speaking. The only sound was the clang of their shoes on the floor. He looked up at his father. His wavy blond hair almost tickled at his ears. Tall and muscular. The female cadets were always fawning over him. Not that he would ever be interested; he had been alone since Louis' mother passed away.

Louis was absorbed in thought when he heard a voice from behind, shouting for his father.

'Captain Andover! A moment!'

They stopped and turned. A small, thin man came scurrying towards them. He was wearing a grey suit that was slightly too big and his greasy hair was slicked back. Captain Andover rolled his eyes as the weasel-faced little man approached. Louis looked at both men, then took his games device out of his pocket.

'Captain Andover, it's a pleasure to finally meet you.' His voice
was squeaky. The captain looked him up and down.

'You're Vincent Stadler aren't you?'

'Yes Captain!'

'Listen Mr Stadler, when my ship leaves this planet I don't want you on it.'

Vincent flinched at the harshness in the Captain's voice. He continued regardless. 'But Captain, my boss has signed my travel docket. He wants me on your Ark and I have every intention of being on it.'

Captain Andover looked Vincent directly in the eye. Stadler had

tried to stand a little taller, but now he cowered beneath the Captain's gaze.

'Look, Mr Stadler, I don't care who signed your docket. If I ever

catch you on my ship, trying to sell life insurance to my crew, I will bounce you out the nearest airlock!'

'Look, I don't see the problem; I just try to offer peace of mind!'

'I'm going to explain this to you as simply as I can. In two weeks from now my crew and I will be on a ship that will be travelling through space at speeds which half the scientists on the planet still insist are impossible. So I don't need you selling contracts to my crew that remind them that they might die on this mission.' He was looking angrier with every word and the increase in volume caught his son's attention. The boy stuffed his game back in his pocket, looked at Vincent Stadler and thought, this guy doesn't stand a chance!

'I'm just trying to present an organised face on all of this!' Vincent was sounding quite desperate. 'I want to make myself useful!'

'Mr Stadler, in the New World a man like you will never be useful. You'd better hope I don't ever catch you on my ship. Louis, come on.'

The captain looked at his son who smiled in return. They continued along the corridor, leaving Vincent looking somewhat forlorn.

They continued in silence along the drab, grey corridor, heading slowly towards the observation room which had been lovingly nicknamed Obs by the teenagers who met up there at night. The silence was thick as they walked, and neither wanted to be the first to break it.

They reached the door to the observation room and walked inside. The room was nice enough considering it was on the north side of the complex. The cleaners never really made it this far and most of the public rooms were covered in graffiti and broken furniture as a result.

The local kids had scribbled their offensive slogans across the walls and had left their rubbish on the floor. The problem was, this room offered the best view, so people would regularly hold their noses and come in to look over the old city below them.

The far wall was made entirely from glass and you could see the whole of New Amerland City. It was spectacular. You could see the old buildings that people had used before the Incident and the roads that they drove along. Everything was grey with dust and the air toxic was so that if you dared to venture outside, you had to make use of the space suits and airlocks that were placed along the wall. The bigger city complexes were connected by tunnels and subways; smaller towns were more dangerous. They weren't as well equipped and people were poisoned by the air every day. They were filled with the Unpleasant Ones, creatures that were once human. Now they were murderous, cannibalistic fiends who prey on those who were forced to use the tunnels.

Louis and his father crossed the room to the window and looked outside. It was dark and dusty out there.

Across the murky cityscape you could just make out the outline of a giant transport, an indefinable shape that towered over the city. It cast its huge shadow over the bleak and empty shells below. The Ark was suspended by scaffolding, and occasionally it swayed precariously in the wind. The finishing touches were being added and it was due to leave Earth in two weeks. Only the richest could afford the outrageous price of a ticket to safety. Those who couldn't afford their place on the Ark had to earn it – a difficult merit that was decided by the aptitude test. Those who failed could only dream of winning the lottery.

The lottery took place every two years, offering out-tickets to those who would otherwise be left to die on the rock they called home. It was a huge affair filled with ceremonies and parties and good spirits. It was televised for those who couldn't afford to go, and tickets were checked against the winning numbers. If you won you were flown over to the biggest city complex in the country, aptly named Utopia. It was clean there, and the pollution level in the air was lower. That usually meant that the dust didn't get into the systems and cause mass shutdowns of things like lighting and atmospheric controls – at New Amerland Complex, they once spent a week in their dark, snowy apartments.

At Utopia they would shower you with gifts and treat you well; you would spend two weeks living in luxury before you were whisked off in the Ark.

'Dad.' Louis barely spoke the word; he was staring intently out the window at the huge ship. 'Is that where we're gonna live now?'

'Yes son. That's the Ark. It's like Earth away from Earth.' It was the Captain's turn to chuckle. 'You'll love it up there. You'll have all the computers and science you can handle.' He smiled at his son.

'What happens to the people that don't get on?'

'Another will be built in two years and they might get on that one.'

'But what if the Earth burns before then?'

The captain took a deep breath and looked at his son. 'Who told you the Earth would burn?'

'Come on Dad, I'm not a baby. I looked it up. The sun is readying itself to go supernova and part of that is an increase in size. As the sun gets bigger its gravity gets stronger. That means that we get pulled closer. Every year, Dad, the Earth gets closer to the sun. How much longer can humans survive on this planet?' Louis looked at his feet.

Clarke stared at his son and wondered when he had become so intelligent and so astute. Something had changed in the boy since his mother's accident and he had become a darker shade of himself. Louis had seen his mother die that day and no child should go through that.

Louis had started walking towards the door. For his age he was a small child, even puny. All the other children were bigger than him but that's probably because he used his pocket money on little bits of computer parts. He enjoyed building miniature robots. He could really see how all things electrical were supposed to work and he used that knowledge to build all sorts of toys. The other boys thought he was weird; they spent all their money on food.

CHAPTER TWO

THE FEET THAT WERE ATTACHED TO THE CEILING were clad in big anti-gravity boots. The legs that were attached to the feet were covered by thick overalls and the rest of the body was hidden behind a great chunk of machinery. Wires kept flying from behind it and bits of steel fell noisily to the metal grid that was the flooring. There was much clanging, and the occasional grunt came from the body that the legs belonged to. There was a definite frustration in the air.

Two young men walked into the room. One was shorter and considerably fatter than the other. His face was slightly pink and he had a thick mass of brown curls tumbling down past his ears and almost touching his neck. He was dressed in the same coloured overalls as the legs above him. The taller of the two looked around the large room with hazel eyes. He had dirty blond hair that was styled neatly in a side parting. His clothes consisted of a shirt and combat pants; the uniform of a navigation officer. He glanced at the floor beneath where the legs were working and frowned. He was a computer man and ships' engines and mechanical bits and pieces didn't really compute. He spotted the boots before his rotund friend.

'Alissa, Is that you up there?'

'Yeah it's me.'

'Will you come down here?'

'I'm a little busy right now Shem. Can it wait?'

'The test starts in an hour!'

There was silence for a few moments, followed by an audible sigh, and then the loud and unmistakable sound of A-G boots clanging down the metal wall. The boots landed on the ground and Alissa bent down to unbuckle them. She stepped out of the boots and stood up straight. Her hair was mousy brown and tied in a knot on the top of her head. Her face was smudged with oil and her overalls were filthy. She wasn't completely unfortunate looking but her chubby physique and grubby appearance meant she wasn't the most sought-after girl around. She grabbed her everyday boots and slipped her feet into them. They clicked themselves into place around her ankles and she jogged over to the guys. 'Okay, let's go.'

'You're not going to get changed? Maybe splash some water on

your face?'

Alissa wiped at her face with her hands, smearing more dirt across her forehead. 'Better?'

'Uhh … sure, you look great.' Shem smiled a little to himself as she walked past him to the door.

'Are you guys nervous?' She pushed a few buttons to open the door. 'I'm scared.' Ham looked sheepishly at his two friends.

'Aw Ham, you don't have to worry. You're gonna do fine. We're all gonna get off this rock.'

Alissa put a reassuring hand on his shoulder as they walked down the hallway.

'What if we don't? What are we going to do if one of us doesn't make it?'

Alissa looked angrily at Shem. 'We'll play the lottery. And if we still don't get on we try again in two years. I guarantee you guys we will all make it off Earth before it burns. Ok?'

She looked at Ham. He seemed less worried already.

***

Four men sat at a table in a darkened room. A spotlight above the table only made everything else appear darker. They all wore black suits and they each wore their hair the same way. There were few distinguishing features between them. One had a small scar underneath his bottom lip, another had a tattoo behind his ear, the third had crystal blue eyes and the fourth wore a silver glove. They sat in silence, staring at each other. Eventually the one with the scar spoke.

'The test is about to begin.'

'It must be closely monitored,' said the one with blue eyes. 'The assassin will be found.'

'What do we do with the sleeper?' asked the tattooed man.

'The sleeper will be killed.' They all looked at the man with the silver glove. He had their attention so he continued. 'The sleeper has fulfilled his duty. He is now a liability. He has death on his hands and can no longer be trusted. He must be disposed of.'

'But his mission is not yet complete!' Blue Eyes rose to his feet.

'The assassin will continue the mission. You have my personal

guarantee.'

Silver Glove turned his gaze back to the table.

***

Ham, Shem and Alissa wandered along a metal corridor with hundreds of others the same age, all heading to the Testing Room. The aptitude test was massively important, designed to pre-select those twenty-five-year-olds who might be capable of manning a star ship.

Ham started to slow down; the others noticed and slowed with him. Alissa looked at him with concern.

'Ham, what's wrong?'

'The enhancement drugs, I gotta take 'em or I'll fail! I don't want to fail!' His eyes welled up as he started to panic. When it came to mental capacity, he was almost childlike.

'Ok Ham, stand behind us and do it.'

Alissa and Shem stood together to hide Ham. After a few seconds he coughed and grunted. Enhancements were not only illegal, they were very unpleasant to take. The powdered drug had to be snorted to be absorbed quickly, but it was slightly corrosive and burned painfully as it worked its way into the bloodstream.

'Are you done?' Shem looked worried.

'Yes.'

The three friends looked at each other, then continued down the corridor in silence. They reached the door of the Testing Room and walked in. It was a massive space filled with single desks, each with a seat and a computer terminal. Hundreds of their peers were already taking their seats and talking amongst themselves. They walked to their respective stations and logged in their details.

'Please place your left hand onto the palm screen for fingerprint recognition.' Came a flat, computer-generated voice. Alissa placed her hand on the screen and a blue light scanned her palm. A small pink flower appeared on the monitor.

'Please focus on the flower for iris recognition.'

The voice was female and it made Alissa wonder why all computer voices were female. As she stared at the monitor the same blue light scanned her eyes. She leaned back in her seat and awaited the start of the test.

Shem looked over at Alissa. She was looking relaxed and he
couldn't understand how she could be so calm while he was feeling so panicked. If they failed this test they'd be stuck here. His attention went to Ham; he looked almost bemused, like this test meant nothing – that was the drugs, that was what they did to you. He didn't like being around Ham when he was enhanced because he became kind of mean, like a professor that talks down to you because you don't understand the material. The computer in front of him flashed up a large, red '10'. The countdown to the test had started.

As the numbers flashed by, Ham stared at the screen. Seven...Six...

Nothing they could ask would be too difficult for him. He could fly through this test with the greatest of ease. He was actually looking forward to it. He wanted to be the first to finish with 100% – easy unless there was another candidate on enhancement drugs. He looked around the room but no one looked as confident as he felt. He smiled to himself and looked back at the screen. The numbers continued to count down...

The four men in suits stared at a screen that was built into the table top in their dark little room. The numbers were counting down on this screen as well. Silver Glove looked at his companions' faces. At zero, the test began. Answers to questions began flickering across their screen, dozens at a time. They could see every answer given by every candidate and their eyes began to flicker and dart with the information.

Alissa leaned closer to her screen. The headset she was wearing irritated her ears. She didn't like it. Her face grew more concerned with every passing question. She hardly understood any of it. She was a mechanic, not a physicist. She started guessing answers.

Shem was looking pleased. This was what he spent his life studying for. He knew the answers. There were a few questions that threw him but he worked them out as best he could and he was pretty sure he was going to pass.

Ham had finished. You could always tell those who were unnaturally gifted because they were the ones who finished first without breaking a sweat. They were the ones people hated. They were the ones on drugs.

The four men in suits were still staring at the screen.
'Candidate 732 has completed the test with 100% accuracy.' Blue Eyes raised his eyebrows, looked at the others in turn. They returned his gaze.
'No,' said Tattoo. He looked back down at the screen. 'He used the enhancement drug. He is not what we are looking for.'
'What are we looking for?' Everyone now looked at Scar Face. 'We need someone with exceptional mental capabilities. We won't get that without the drugs.'
'The most dangerous assassin is the one with nothing to lose. We need the most desperate candidate. The one that fails will be the one we want.' Silver Glove sat back down in his seat and looked at the other men. 'If you

take someone who has passed and earned their passage on the ship, they will turn their back on us. They cannot be trusted. If you take someone who has failed and is therefore stranded here until the lottery smiles upon them, they will be more likely to be coerced into doing their duty.'

***

'Thank you for taking the test. Have a great today!'

Alissa stared at the computer screen, which was now blank. The test was over and she had known only a handful of answers. She took a deep breath and fought with the tears that threatened to give her away. As she stood up Ham and Shem came walking over. Shem had a wide grin plastered across his face.

'I knew it,' he said. 'Well, most of it. I thought question twelve was gonna get me but then I remembered, when multiplying integers you have to multiply the absolute values and use the rules to determine the sign of the answer. Then it's just obvious.'

'Of course it is.' Alissa produced the best smile she could muster.

She turned to Ham. 'How are you feeling? Are the drugs wearing off?'

'Yeah, my head kinda hurts a bit. Nothing too bad though.'

'Your nose is bleeding.' Alissa's fake smile disappeared and she pulled an oily tissue out of her pocket and offered it to him. He took it gratefully and pressed it hard against his nose.

'You have to stop with the drugs now Ham. You passed the test. You don't need them anymore.'

Shem watched as his best friend stood before him with one hand pressed to his temple and the other stuffing a dirty tissue up his nose. The sight made him deeply sad and he didn't quite know why.

'I can't stop now! I gotta keep takin' them! They think I can work on the Ark but I can't. I don't have that kind of brain. Not like you Shem. No, I gotta take 'em or they'll throw me off the ship or something.' Ham was definitely returning to his normal state.

'I'll help you. So will Alissa. We'll all be there together anyway.
There's no way you'll get thrown off.' Alissa looked down as Shem talked. 'I think we should all go to Saime's for drinks! We made it through the test, this is a happy occasion.'

Shem led the way to the door. Ham followed close behind, massaging his temple and checking to see if the bleeding had subsided. Alissa walked slowly behind them, thinking about the test. Maybe I should've taken the drugs too. She felt like she'd made a huge mistake because you only get one chance at the aptitude test, and she'd blown it.

CHAPTER THREE

'ONE DAY, SON, YOU'LL BE A STAR SHIP CAPTAIN   just like me. Wouldn't you like that?'

The man looked down at his son, who was staring at the brilliant blue sky.

'Yes Father.' His dark, deep-set eyes and mop of brown hair seemed to accentuate the pallor of his skin. He didn't really want to be there.

'You can explore the galaxy, with a crew to follow your every order.' The man seemed oblivious to his son's discomfort. He stood towering over the child with his chest puffed out. People often wondered how such an impressive man had spawned such a small, sickly boy.

'To become a rich and famous icon is your destiny, my son. You know, not just anyone can become a captain. You have to be strong, and clever, and most importantly have someone like me to vouch for you.' The man puffed out his chest even further while the boy looked at the floor.

'Yes Father.'

Garret's eyes flickered open and he looked at the bare ceiling. It was still dark outside but that didn't mean much in the complex. Every city in the world was set to Utopia's time which meant you could be eating your breakfast at nine o'clock at night. It was an unusual way to live. His dream about his father had forced Garret awake in the middle of the night. He always found dreaming about one's past to be rather clichéd but without the sleep drugs he was a slave to his subconscious. He sat upright in his bed and swung his legs around to the floor. He rubbed his eyes and stood up. Garret always stood up straight. It was something his mother had instilled in him as a child.

So even now, fifty years later, in the middle of the night, half awake and with aching joints, he stood up straight. He wandered into the bathroom. Sat down on the toilet and rested his head in his hands. How had the world changed so much?

He remembered the day the first bomb had fallen. He had spent the morning with his mother in the parks. A beautiful day. They'd had a picnic on a hill, like something out of a picture book, the grass vivid and green. They even had a white and red gingham blanket, and they ate ham sandwiches and crisps. His mother wanted to run some errands and sent him home to play, not that he had anyone to play with – he had no friends, but he had his books and he loved to read. He gave his mother a quick hug and turned to go home. That was the last time he saw her. When he arrived home he was walking up the stairs when he felt the faintest tremor beneath his feet. He had been terrified and his father had appeared on the run and grabbed him and dragged him to the shelter below their house. They were safe there from the explosions and the fallout.

They stayed down there for months, living on their rations. His father had known that this was coming and he had enough money to make a survival plan...

Garret stood up and walked over to the sink, resting his hands on either side of the plastic basin. He looked in the mirror and turned on the tap. He never made it to captain but he never wanted to. He was a first officer and damn proud of it. It was the rebellion against his father that he cherished most, the look on the old man's face when he told him he was refusing the offer of command. He splashed water on his face and took a deep breath; the memory of his dream was beginning to fade and he felt tired enough to try to go back to sleep.

He made his way back to the bed and sat down. He felt tired and old. Wasn't it time for him to retire? I could never do it. I love space too much. He had gotten his newest assignment through the post. The Ark – a simple mission. Take a bunch of people who are desperate to escape and fly them round the galaxy to the New World. He would be under the command of Captain Andover.

They'd never met but Garret knew him by reputation; he was a good captain, or so he'd heard. He wasn't particularly excited about the mission, but he was glad to get off the planet again because he slept so much better in space. He rested his head on the pillow and closed his eyes. Without the sleep drugs he would be plagued by emotional dreams, but he was so tired. He started to drift off. Suddenly his computer whirred into life. It emitted a loud ringing sound that thrust Garret back into the waking world just as he was drifting back off to sleep. He sat up and swore, made his way to the terminal. He sat down and looked at the screen. He pressed a few buttons and a face appeared. 'Garret.' The man on the screen was young. Too young, thought Garret.

'We have some information about your mission.'

'Go on.'

'I'm sending you the passenger and crew manifests for the Ark.

You'll have access to all the identity cards.'

'Thank you.'

'Not a problem, Sir. Have a good today.' Garret clicked on silent and went back to bed.

CHAPTER FOUR

ALISSA KNOCKED BACK A SHOT OF SOMETHING THAT might once have been whiskey and shuddered as it burned its way down her throat. She sat on a scummy stool, resting her arms on a sticky metal bar top. She was a regular at Saime's little bar; it was a bit of a dive but the drinks were cheap and money was an issue. Her eyes trailed round the room, blurring her surroundings and making her feel more than a little queasy. The room was lit with red lights and the furnishings were all metal which made the place look sharper than it really was. This is where the poorer people came to relax at the end of their long shifts.

The majority of seats were taken up by people in overalls drinking and chatting loudly to each other. Laughter was abundant in here and everyone was usually in good spirits.

Alissa leant her head on her arms and closed her eyes as the room started to spin. She wanted to shut it all out. The barman was staring at her, wondering whether she was too drunk to stay. He decided he'd serve her at least one more before he threw her out. She opened her eyes and looked over at Ham and Shem who were sitting at a table, drunkenly discussing metaphysics which would be an unusual sight for any other time of day. After all, Ham knew nothing about metaphysics, but when he was drunk he considered himself to be quite the authority on all things scientific. It didn't matter that most of the things he said were complete rubbish – Shem was usually too drunk to correct him. It was amusing though, two men talking at each other, neither hearing a word the other was saying. Alissa smiled to herself and then thought: in two weeks, I'll never see my best friends again.

The thought of losing them broke her heart and her eyes started to sting with the tears she was holding back.

When she had met Ham she had been an altogether quieter girl, with neither friends nor family. Since then she had gotten quite used to spending time with her colleagues and smiling her way through the day. But at night, when she was alone, her mind would play through the conversations she'd had and she would wish they came to more; what she wanted were real friendships. Then she met Ham and everything changed. They had been working at the New Amerland Complex together on the exhaust ports for a mining ship when they had struck up a conversation. Alissa realised within minutes that Ham wasn't quite right with the things he said but his hands moved around a ship's mechanics like nothing she'd ever seen and they talked all day while they worked. She enjoyed the feeling she got when he committed to the conversation as much as she did.

He told her that he lived in a smaller complex a few miles over, next to his best friend, but they were being transferred to New Amerland so they could go up with The Hawk. Alissa had heard of the ship – it was designed to spot small areas on planets that could be mined for minerals. When he returned he'd be living two hallways over from Alissa and they'd work together every day in the mechanics' bay. The five months that he was away were the longest of her life and she counted every second as she waited for his return.

On the day he was due back she decorated her room with coloured plastic sheeting from the garage and ordered some food from the canteen. They sent her thick cabbage soup and some hard bread and while it wasn't luxury, it was home. He arrived exactly when he said he would, her little doorbell ringing through her quarters to announce his arrival. She ran to her door, pressed the buttons on the panel and as soon as it opened she flung her arms around his neck. He hugged her back with a childlike enthusiasm and lifted her right off her feet.

Once he'd put her down she notice the tall mad standing behind him.

'This is Shem, he's my best friend too!'

Shem smiled politely and offered his hand; she shook it and smiled right back. The three of them stood on the threshold awkwardly until she ushered them inside for food.

They hadn't been apart since.

Alissa stood up and staggered across the crowded bar. She had taken a shower since the aptitude test and taken her hair out of the knot, allowing it to fall past her shoulders. She kept her eyes on the floor because she didn't trust them not to spout tears and give her away; she didn't like for people to see her upset, and it embarrassed her because tears were weakness. Her hair fell over her face and she didn't push it away; instead she pushed open a heavy door and fell through. It led to the airlock that in turn led outside. For one short second she considered running outside just to see if it really was that bad, just to see how quickly she'd die, but instead she slumped to the floor and allowed her tears to fall. She was obscenely drunk and falling deeper and deeper into an emotional hole and as she fell her thoughts swam around in her mind and she found it difficult to make sense of anything. Visions of her father mixed with Ham like some strange combination of young and old, thoughtful and commanding. The room continued to spin beneath her as she tried to shift the grotesque image from her brain.

***

The morning came all too quickly for Louis; he opened his eyes and stared at his grey ceiling. He'd been dreaming about beautiful blue skies with puffy white clouds that sat like marshmallows in the sky. It was a nice dream that reminded him of the Holo-Chambers he visited with his father and the happier times they spent there. He sat up in bed and looked around his room. He really loved it. It was his; somewhere he could be completely alone and do whatever he wanted. He was never wrong in his room and sometimes he liked to pretend that he was the king and all his toys were loyal subjects who did as he commanded.

He stood up and noticed how squishy and soft his blue carpet really was. When I get on the Ark I'll never feel this carpet under my toes again. He kept noticing things like that. He ran his fingers across the smooth, creamy coloured wall – he had drawn many pictures over the years with his favourite crayons and the best ones made it onto the wall. He turned and walked over to his drawers. There was a teddy sitting on them that he'd had since he was a baby. He picked it up. 'People keep telling me that ten is too old for teddies. But I don't think so.' He held the bear in his arms as his eyes travelled round the room.

He had shelves on his walls that were filled with little metallic gadgets. He had built them all. There were little robots that scuttled around on ten spindly legs, little boxes that showed cute pictures along to music. And his personal favourite, the companion. It was a device he was working on that could communicate with people. It was essentially some circuitry and a speaker, but if you put it inside a toy – a bear for instance – that bear would be able to talk to you. It would seem completely sentient. Or at least that was the idea. Unfortunately he could never get it to work and it had been consigned to the shelf. But every now and again he would take it over to his little desk and fiddle around with the wires.

He tossed his bear onto the bed, sighed deeply and walked out of the room. He wandered towards the bathroom to brush his teeth but when he got to the hallway he heard his father's voice. He abandoned his bathroom visit and instead made his way to the door of the living area where his father stood in front of his terminal looking remarkable angry. 'What makes you think your opinion counts? I don't want him on my ship!'

'Listen Captain, this world is all about material possession.' The man on the screen was a fat, balding man with a flop sweat.

'The rumours about the end of the world are just that, rumours. Now imagine for a second that you are in my shoes. I have an opportunity here to make a lot of money and I don't intend on passing that up! Stadler is one of my best salesmen and the first of my company to be on an Ark. He will be the first man on the New World to sell life insurance. I will have one hundred percent of the business and I'll make a goddamn fortune.'

'Listen, Mr Chalmers, your man will not be on my ship. Do I make myself clear? You don't control the manifest, I do. So have yourself a fine today.'

Clarke pressed a few buttons and the screen bleeped and went blank. He stood silently for a moment, reflected on the conversation and decided on his next course of action, which at this particular moment was breakfast. He turned towards the door and noticed Louis. He walked across the lino flooring into the kitchen.

'Okay Lou, what's up?'

'I don't wanna go.' Louis sat at the dining room table. It was a beautiful dark hardwood piece so it stood out in a room that was mainly beige. His father was not a colourful man. Clarke looked at his son. 'Why not?'

'I like it here.' Louis picked at a splinter on the table top. 'Why can't we stay?'

'Son we've been through this.' He sat himself at the table across from the child. 'It'll be a better life for us out there, and I'll make sure of that. I know you're scared. And if you want to know the truth, I am too. But I am your father and I will protect you over everything else. Do you understand? Nothing will be able to hurt you.'

'I understand.'

'Good. And you know, you can bring a lot of your stuff with you so you need to do some packing. Now, do you want some breakfast?'

Louis nodded so Clarke stood up again and walked over to the fridge. 'We have some lovely looking fake bacon? I could toast up some bread?'

'That sounds good, Dad.' Louis got up and wandered towards the door. 'Where you headed, kid?'

'Bathroom!'

CHAPTER FIVE

SHEM COULDN'T UNDERSTAND WHERE ALISSA WAS. they always met up for breakfast before their shifts. He looked at Ham, who was staring at the food menu above their heads. The canteen was an unusual-looking place. It was a large room stuffed full of little metal tables surrounded by little metal chairs. It was always difficult to move between them, you had to squeeze your way through, but even with all that furniture it was almost impossible to find a seat. The hall was always packed full of people because it was the safest place to eat. It was a regulation canteen which meant they could only serve government-approved food, which also meant it was a vegetarian menu. Animals couldn't be classed as food anymore. Most of them died during the Incident and those that survived were altered by the fallout so anyone with any sense in New Amerland ate at this canteen. Except the rich, of course – they could afford to keep a store of food at home.

'I'm gonna get fake bacon and potatoes,' Ham said hungrily. Shem looked at the door to the canteen.

'Where's Alissa?' His face was etched with worry. They hadn't seen her since the drunken night at the bar and while he assumed the hangover had kept her in bed most of the next day he couldn't account for her prolonged disappearance, and she was going to miss her shift if she didn't turn up soon, and that just wasn't like her.

'I bet she's sick. People get sick sometimes, Shem.'

'Yeah I know. It's just … She usually tells us.' Shem joined the queue for food and Ham looked over at him. 'If she's not here by lunch then we can go to her quarters. If you want to.'

'Yeah, okay. Let's do that.' Satisfied that he could speak to her

later, Shem looked at the menu and decided on cabbage risotto. They moved along with the queue and had their food unceremoniously dumped onto their trays by the fat woman behind the counter.

They made their way along the line, looking at the feeble bits of fruit that sat in a bowl. Fruit and vegetables were gown in hydroponic centres and each complex provided enough for its residents. The only problem with the system, thought Shem, was that if you lived in a complex dedicated to machinery and the like, it was unlikely the hydroponic centre would grown anything more than some dry old apples and the odd banana, none of which looked very appetising sitting in sterilised metal bowls.

They continued on and reached the pay station behind which sat an ancient woman who looked like she should've been put out to pasture a long time ago. She looked exactly like what a dinner lady should look like. She had her hair in a net, big jam jar glasses, a greasy-looking white pinafore and a burning cigarette hanging out of her mouth. Granted the cigarette would've been frowned upon before the Incident but health and safety wasn't considered that big an issue anymore and smoking was generally allowed anywhere in the complex.

Shem handed some notes to the decrepit old woman, just enough to cover his and Ham's breakfasts, and then they turned and scanned the room for empty seats. Ham spotted two together and made a run for it while Shem followed behind. By the time he had made his way to a filthy table in the corner of the room, Ham had already sat down. It seemed quite possible to Shem that in the thirty years it had stood in this spot, the table had never been cleaned.

Ham stabbed a potato with his fork and jammed it whole into his mouth. Shem looked with mild disgust at the man he called his best friend.

'What you got planned for this shift?' Ham spat the words through the potato he was chewing.

'Computer stuff.' Shem smiled. He really loved his job. 'I'm helping to programme the personality into the Ark's computer. They think it's good for the systems to understand people so they try to make them more human. It's just a voice, of course, but it'll be friendly. It'll also be the first male computer personality ever to be on a star ship. It's pretty neat.'

'Wow. What's his name?' Ham was beginning to look interested.

'His name? He doesn't have a name.'

'How can he not have a name? You're givin' him a personality; you gotta give him a name!'

'I suppose.' Shem stared at his rice. 'How do you name a
computer?'

'Well, what is it he does?'

'He's in control of navigation operations and habitation.'

'So...' Ham's face contorted into a frown. He was concentrating hard. 'NOAH!' he cried.

'What?' It was Shem's turn to be confused.

'NOAH' repeated Ham. 'Navigation Operations and Habitation.
N.O.A.H.'

Shem stared at him for a few seconds and then broke into a smile.

'Ham, you are a genius. It's perfect!'

'I know.' Ham puffed out his chest; he was clearly very proud of himself. Then he stabbed his fork into another potato and stuffed it into his mouth. He almost spat it out when a plastic tray clattered onto the table beside him. Alissa turned the chair side-on to the table and plonked herself down on it and smiled at her friends.

She looked pale, her hair was falling down over her shoulders and her clothes were dishevelled. She had a bowl of oats and water and she was stuffing it into her mouth hungrily.

'Hey Alissa, you okay there?'
Shem was genuinely concerned. Alissa looked up from her food and smiled. She swallowed a mouthful. 'I'm good. Great in fact.

Hungry, though.' She stuffed more food into her mouth as Ham and Shem watched.

'So, we haven't seen you since Saturday night. Hung over, were we?'

Alissa looked at him, confused. 'Hung over? We were drinking?'

'Ah, no. Me and Ham were drinking. You practically went
swimming in a bottle of the old firewater.'

'I don't remember.' Alissa scraped the spoon along the bottom of her metal bowl and raised it to her mouth; that's when she realised it was empty. She put the spoon down and looked up at her friends. 'I guess I drank more than I thought.' She smiled.

An alarm sounded. It was the signal to start the working day so the three friends picked up their empty trays and walked over to a large hatch in the wall, threw in the trays in and headed towards the door, talking to each other about nothing in particular.

Once they left the canteen they followed the hallway and when they reached the end they separated. Shem headed towards the Navigation Wing while Ham and Alissa walked to the garages.

'I passed the test.'

Alissa looked at the floor. 'You got your results, huh?'

'Yep. Didn't you?'

'Yeah, I passed.' She wasn't going to admit what she had seen on her results sheet. It was just too humiliating.

'So we both passed.' Ham looked pleased. 'And Shem too! That means we go on the Ark together!'

Alissa still couldn't look at him. 'So, what's the plan for today?'

'We gotta help rebuild the shuttle that crashed last month. They want to know where it came from and if we can use it.'

'Oh yeah, I heard about that, some people think it's alien don't they?' Alissa paused for a minute, looking thoughtful. 'I guess we're gonna find out.'

***

The subway systems in New Amerland were death traps, the cars themselves like giant tin cans, with no seating and a limited number of rails to hold on to. People died in the cars so often that it had become commonplace. It was seen as a sign of stupidity to die on the subway and very little sympathy was given to those who succumbed to that particular fate.

The usual cause of death was an old fashioned crushing under the weight of bodies, but there were a lucky few who managed to fall out of the open doors and give a spectacular six hundred and fifty volt show, like disgusting red fireworks exploding against the wall. The subway was the scariest mode of transportation, but a necessary evil that must be contended with in order to reach the accommodations, often quite far from the heart of the complex.

***

Garret learned a long time ago that if you wanted to survive the subway journey you had to be first in line to board. You wanted to avoid being too close to the sides and doors. You had to manoeuvre yourself into the middle and use the rail that ran down the centre of the car. The people that surrounded you cushioned you and as long as you didn't get trapped against the wall you'd be fine.

He waited as the first two cars passed, then strode confidently to the edge of the platform. As soon as the doors opened he walked inside and positioned himself in the centre under the handrail. He held onto it as the space around him diminished and was filled by an urgent, crushing mass of people in all shapes and sizes, among them a skinny young woman and a rather large sweaty man who managed to press himself hard against him. It was not a pleasant experience.

The journey was a long one, and for most of the way Garret thought about his life, and how it had come to this. I am a rich man, he thought; why do I still have to travel on this infernal contraption? There was, in fact, no real answer and for that reason he would be grateful to get off this planet.

He was sometimes glad his mother had died in the Incident because she was a slight and rather gentle woman, with delicate features and a soft voice. He couldn't imagine her on the subway or trying to traverse the tunnels that connected parts of the complex. Then he hated himself for being grateful for her death.

The subway train pulled up at the station. It was the last stop before the return journey. The subway car had emptied quite a lot since he boarded and he moved towards the door, stepping over the crushed and mangled body of a young man who must have lost his footing and fallen during the ride.

He walked out onto the station platform and took a deep breath. Many years ago there would have been stairs leading up to the street. Not anymore though – all subways were closed in to protect those who dared to travel. He walked to the archway that led to Swan Towers, an apartment building south of the main complex. It was in the upper price range but only by a hair; some people called it nice, but that was only in comparison to their hovels.

He walked along a tunnel that led towards the lift. It was dark and grimy with stone walls and the occasional light. It smelled bad and it was always damp, but it was the same with all the underground tunnels. He reached the lift and pressed the button and after a few moments the big metal door opened and he stepped inside.

There was graffiti on the walls, and he looked absently at the obscene scribbling as he pressed the button for the top floor and waited. The big metal doors slid closed and the lift moved upwards. He looked at the numbers above the doors and watched as the dial slowly turned.

He spent the journey upwards humming a tune to no one in particular. It was a familiar tune – he didn't know where he had heard it before he knew he hadn't made it up. He always thought it was amusing that he could focus so intently on something that had no relevance at all to his life and as a smile broke across his face, the lift reached the top floor of the building and the door slid open to reveal a long hallway. Painted an unusual shade of yellow, it was supposed to be soothing, probably, he thought, because if you lived in this era you needed to be soothed.

As he stepped out of the lift the door slammed shut behind him, making him jump. The circuitry was old and the doors don't glide like they used to. He walked down the hall, looking closely at each door on the way and noting the numbers. He found the one he was looking for, and standing in front of it he realised that it looked like all the other doors. Nothing about it was special, nothing screamed 'Important!' like he thought it should, in fact the only difference was the number.

Garret rang the bell and waited. After standing awkwardly for a few moments, he heard noises on the other side of the door, and it slid open with a whoosh to reveal a handsome man in his late thirties.

'Captain Andover, I presume?' Garret offered his hand and it was taken.

'Yeah that's me. You can call me Clarke you know.'

'I know, Captain, but I'd really prefer not to.' The captain smiled and nodded. 'I understand. Please, come in.'

He stepped to the side to reveal his apartment. Garret walked past him and looked around. It was nice alright; what was lacking in the hallway was made up for in abundance in this room alone.

The living space was quite large, bigger than those provided in the staff quarters of the complex. Garret's was about a quarter of the size.

Maybe I made a mistake in my career choice, he thought grimly. There were big squashy-looking chairs against one wall, half-turned to face each other, with a little table in between. It looked like a place for intimate chats. On the adjoining wall was a long sofa, as over-stuffed as the chairs. It beckoned to Garret to throw himself upon it and curl up in its thick folds.

Facing the sofa, attached to the wall, was a large screen that he assumed was used for communicating with the base of operations for the Ark missions, and no doubt personal calls as well.

The place was clean – unusual for a man in this day and age. Garret stood open-mouthed, taking in the opulence, and the Captain's voice made him jump.

'Let's go through to the study to talk.'

Clarke motioned for Garret to follow him and they walked out of the living area into a small hallway, no less beautiful than the previous room, and headed towards the door at the end. There were rooms down one side of the hall and Garret glanced into each one as they passed.

There was the kitchen and dining room, from which emanated delicious smells. Garret's quarters did not boast a kitchen; his dining was done at the cafeteria in the complex.

They passed the Captain's bedroom, and Garret tried to sneak a look but the door was only ajar. Next, the bathroom and then what looked like a child's bedroom.

They reached the door at the end of the hall and Clarke opened it to reveal his study. This was a room he was obviously proud of. Huge windows along an entire wall revealed the best view that New Amerland had to offer.

It wasn't much to look at when you were at ground level, thought Garret, but from up here it was really spectacular. You could see the Ark, dominating the skyline, drawing your eye no matter where you tried to direct your gaze.

To his left was an imposing bookcase blocking the wall behind it almost completely, and the most amazing thing was, it was filled with real books. Garret loved to read but it was especially difficult to get your hands on actual books. So these are the perks of the job, he thought.

The floor had a thick shag pile carpet that really invited you to kick off your shoes and dance around on it. But Garret was not the dancing type, and through all of these spectacular visual morsels, the one thing that really commanded attention was the desk. It stood, dark and impressive, in front of the window, mahogany with gold and pearl inlets swirling an intricate pattern around the edge, and behind it was a large executive chair covered in deep red leather.

Garret was quite shocked: leather was rare nowadays. The damn thing must've cost a fortune, he said to himself, with just a tinge of bitterness. There was a smaller chair in front of the desk and this was obviously where Garret was expected to sit. He eyed it suspiciously. It certainly didn't look as inviting as the captain's seat, but Garret made his decision about all of that a long time ago.

Clarke walked around the desk and plonked himself on his leather chair, and his first officer slowly and deliberately walked to the smaller seat and gently placed himself upon it.

'So tell me, Garret. How do you feel about this mission?' The

Captain's eyes were piercing into Garret, looking for any reason to rid himself of the old man.

'I look forward to getting off the planet, Sir.'

'Do you believe the rumours about the planet burning?'

It was a topic hotly debated among scientists everywhere. It was believed by some that the Earth would fall into a new orbit around the sun and even though it was expanding, the gigantic star that gave them life would last millennia. The Ark Program was run by those who believed that everyone was going to die and it was going to be soon.

Garret looked thoughtful for a moment before he said carefully, 'I don't believe them to be rumours, Sir.'

'Of course not, Garret. We've all been brought up to know that the Earth is slowly getting closer to the sun and that within the next ten to twenty years, the planet will be too hot for humans to survive.'

'That is the reason for the Ark Program, is it not, Captain? To go to the New World and continue the human race.'

The captain's face darkened. 'Garret, we're heading into space soon. And we will be travelling further than anyone has before us.

Each Ark has followed a different route so far to give the human race the best chance of finding a planet.'

Garret looked at Clarke, the confusion clear in his face. 'But

Captain, I thought ...'

'That a planet had already been colonised? Well, that was the plan, but things changed. The first Ark, the one that left ten years ago, never found a planet. None of the

Arks that have followed since have found a planet. I don't know what happened to those men and women but I know that this is our chance, Garret, our chance to save humanity. We may need to lay down our lives for the mission. Are you prepared for that?'

We may need to lay down our lives for the mission … The words swirled in Garret's head. This was a babysitting mission, this was supposed to be simple, and here he sat listening to the Captain's words and wishing he was brave enough to stay behind.

'The mission is what matters, Captain.' The words fell out of his mouth before he could stop them.

'You really are your father's son, Garret.' The captain smiled.

'So I've heard. Captain.'

Garret rose to his feet and saluted the captain, who in turn stood to face him and nodded his head.

'You're dismissed Garret.'

He walked out of the apartment and as the door slid shut behind him he closed his eyes. The captain knew something was wrong. This was never meant to be a deadly mission; so how had it become one?

He swallowed hard but his mouth was as dry. He was scared. This was what fear felt like – he didn't experience it often but he didn't need to, because his missions were straightforward and simple. He pressed his thumb and forefinger hard into his eyes and felt betrayed by his tears.

I'm a goddamn coward.

CHAPTER SIX

HANGAR 21 WAS A HUGE OPEN SPACE FILLED WITH mini-ships, so named because they only had a crew of two or three and they were usually assigned to transporting people from the surface of the planet to whatever large craft was waiting for them in orbit.

Some were new and shiny and ready to go straight out into space. They were ships to be proud of, and their owners usually were. Others weren't quite so immaculate; the ship Alissa was standing behind was one such specimen. With its dented outer hull and cracked windows it would be easy to mistake it for a wreck. It was beat up and old and all the paintwork had been burned off in the crash that had brought it to their attention.

Ham was holding back a heavy panel that was hiding a huge circuit board. Alissa had her arms in the hole up to her shoulders and her face was screwed up in concentration.

'I can't reach it, Ham. Can you open the panel up wider please?'

'I'll try.'

Ham pulled harder and Alissa squeezed her entire upper body into the hole, which wasn't the easiest of tasks due to her ample frame. But she was committed now. She might as well see it through.

'I need some light down here!'

'She needs light!' yelled Ham at the top of his voice, and a small man in overalls came rushing over with a torch which he switched on and thrust into the small gap between the panel and Alissa's ribs.

'Oh this is amazing!' Her voice echoed from somewhere beyond the mass of circuitry.

'What is it Alissa? What do you see?' Ham was breaking out in a sweat and his muscles were complaining. The panel was heavy and he was struggling.

'I've never seen anything like this. It's ... it's not from Earth, that's for sure. Move your arm!'

The little man pulled his arm out of the gap and Alissa pushed herself backwards and half fell out of the hole. She found her balance just in time to stop herself from toppling. Ham released the panel and it dropped back into place with a loud clang.

'Okay Miss Namaah, what did you see?'

Her superior was suddenly beside her. Alissa rubbed her face and took a deep breath.

'I don't know. It was weird. Nothing like our technology; highly complex. Whatever it was, it wasn't built by us.'

'Thank you, miss. You do realise that this is classified, of course. To repeat it will get you thrown in the nearest cell. Or worse.'

'Yes, Sir.' Alissa saluted the officer.

'Good work. Keep it up.' He turned and walked away to give his report to the supervisor.

'Okay you guys, you heard the man, let's get the next panel open.'

Ham walked over to it and pulled out his tools. He started cutting into the metal with a laser tool. The ship's electronics were failing and all the power was being diverted to the central core. There was no obvious reason for it, and so far he and Alissa had been unable to determine its purpose.

The look of concentration on his face as the laser sliced through molten metal was obvious; this was a man who should not be disturbed.

'Ham, have you ever met the captain?' Alissa was sitting on a tool box, watching him work. Ham frowned slightly, said something under his breath and turned off the laser. She was always doing this, talking to him when he needed to focus. She didn't understand.

'Alissa, I gotta cut this open dead carefully. I struggle to concentrate you know. It's not easy like it is for you.'

'Ham, you can do this in your sleep, you're better than anyone I know.' There was no condescension in her tone, just admiration for his skill. It always bumped his confidence when she talked to him like that. Ham smiled to himself and turned back to the panel. He lifted the laser saw and continued to cut. 'What about the captain?'

'I mean, what's he like? I've seen pictures of course, everyone has. He's kind of pretty. In a really manly way, you know? I wonder if he's single …' Her voice trailed off while she imagined what it would be like to be the captain's lady.

'His wife died in a horrible accident.' The nonchalant way in which Ham delivered this news to Alissa shocked her. He did this sometimes, he didn't realise what he was saying, didn't realise the connotations.

'I didn't know he was ever married. I wonder what she looked like.' Alissa lay back on the box. 'I bet she was beautiful, and glamorous. The captain would be with someone with class.'

'Actually she was a technician on board the Endeavour.'

'The mining ship?'

'Yeah, I was on there for a few months, remember. She was nice. A little weird, but nice. She took care of me.'

'Jeez Ham, I had no idea! Did you ever meet the captain?'

'No, but she talked about him. They had a kid too, a little boy. Don't know what happened to him though.'

Alissa sat up. 'What do you mean? Isn't he at the school?' Ham shook his head. 'Nope, after she died the kid disappeared. Some people think he was killed in the accident too, but others think

the captain killed him.' Alissa drew in her breath sharply. How could anyone murder their own son?

'Do you think he ... he killed him?'

'No, I think he was just scared, so the captain keeps him with him all the time. That's what I would've wanted.'

Alissa sat quietly and watched Ham work; she didn't know what to say to him when he brought up his family. They had all taken previous Arks and left the planet. They had left their youngest son behind because he was too difficult to deal with. He would be Alissa's responsibility forever – she knew that and it made her swell with pride.

He had become a wonderful man and she was partly to thank, along with Shem.

***

Vincent Stadler sat in a cramped, stuffy office with his fat, bald boss. He picked sullenly at a loose thread on the arm of the chair as his boss glared at him in silence.

This unsettled Vincent; he didn't like this feeling of not knowing. He didn't know what Mr Chalmers wanted from him anymore and he certainly didn't think the current situation was his fault. So he continued to stare at the hole in the chair that his probing fingers were gradually widening, as his boss watched on, unable to hide his irritation.

'Stadler.' The boss's voice was scratchy and deep and it penetrated Vincent's thoughts, causing him to finally make eye contact with his sweaty superior. 'How do you propose we get you on the Ark?'

'I don't know, Sir.' Vincent spat the words through gritted teeth. His boss got to his feet and walked around the room. It was quite obvious to Vincent that he was trying to make himself seem important, that this was how he imagined corporate bosses conducted their dressing-downs. Vincent would have given anything to switch positions and tell his boss exactly what thoughts crept around his greasy little mind. Chalmers waddled over to the door and closed it.

The office was tacky, filled with little golden trinkets that rested on fake mahogany bookcases, the walls were a deep blood red and had awful paintings mounted in cheap, gold-plated frames. There was one item of real value, a beautiful Persian rug given to Chalmers by a travelling man with no name, or at least that's the story he recalled at his parties in front of strangers that didn't care.

The boss waddled back across the room and sat down behind his desk. He stared until eventually Vincent looked up and met his eye. Vincent shifted uncomfortably in his chair while the fat man continued to stare.

'We could try the captain again, or the first officer?' Vincent wasn't enthused by his own idea.

'Don't be ridiculous. The captain refuses to speak to me and his first officer is bound to be in his pocket by now. No, we need something better. We need to get you a job on there.'

Vincent felt the dread in the pit of his stomach. 'But Sir,' he said. 'I failed the aptitude test years ago! I don't know anything about the workings of a spacecraft.'

'That won't matter. For sure, the captain will figure it all out pretty quickly, but my hope is that you're already in space when he does.'

The boss opened a drawer and pulled out a bottle of whiskey and a glass. He upturned the bottle and poured himself a large measure.

'I very much doubt he'll throw you out in the middle of space.' He chuckled and drained the glass he was holding; all the while scrutinizing Vincent's from across the desk. He loved this. He could taste Vincent's disdain and revelled in the fact that the little weasel daren't say a word to him. He cleared his throat loudly and continued.

'There is a man you need to contact. Word has just been sent to him advising him that he has received the promotion he always wanted. His new-found power will go to his head and he will put you onto his crew manifest, as long as you can convince him that you're important enough to get on the damn ship. Do not let me down again, Stadler.'

***

Garret pressed a few buttons and the door to the library slid open with a familiar whoosh. He walked into the large space and eyed up the terminals. Since books were very difficult to get hold of, the library was filled with computer displays allowing the inhabitants of the complex to access the whole of the remaining literary world any time they desired.

The room was grey, mainly because most public rooms were grey. It was the most depressing colour, in Garret's opinion. He walked over to a vacant station and sat down at the terminal. His fingers danced along the keyboard in front of him and the screen hummed into life. He began his search. The captain had told him something unnerving and he needed proof.

'The first Ark, the one that left ten years ago, never found a planet. None of the Arks that have followed since have found a planet.' He turned the words over and over in his mind and he felt sick to his stomach; he had been unable think about anything else.

He had travelled back from the Captain's home without even noticing what was around him. He found himself wandering the drab metallic halls of the complex until he reached the library. If all the Arks so far have failed, something, somewhere will have record of it. It's not that he doubted the captain; but this was something he needed to see with his own eyes.

His search began fruitlessly. All the records said that the previous Arks had reached the New World and that the colonists had been building a life there ever since. After many hours of searching Garret learned that the colonists were referring to themselves as New Worlders (which he thought was ridiculous) and had built a complex to live in, complete with schools, infirmaries and police stations. Bitter thoughts flowed through his mind about the people that had sat and written these lies. Did they know the truth? That all those people were now just floating through space, perhaps clinging to the hope of survival?

His eyes flickered across the screen as he pulled up more stories, stuff about the schools being even better than on Earth, children learning faster and the future of mankind looking brighter than ever before.

Garret stood up and turned his back to the computer. There was nothing here. Whatever the captain knew was obviously secret and would probably land them both in trouble if whoever gave that information to Clarke found out he'd confided in his first officer. He left the library and headed back to his quarters.

***

Alissa left the hangar alone. She'd not felt that well today and her mind kept wandering, taking her back to the aptitude test and reminding her of her failure. Ham had decided to stay late to work on reattaching the panels. Alissa told herself, you're not going to work late anymore – after all, it looks like you've got the rest of your life to work in this damned overblown garage.

She wandered down the corridor to the main door out of the engineering department. Her fingers traced the security number on the panel and the door slid open to reveal Shem, hand raised to the door panel, ready to open it. He gave her a smile and she returned it as best she could.

'Hey Shem, what brings you to my neck of the woods?'

'Ham called. I'm gonna go keep him company while he works. You heading home?'

'Yeah, I guess. I may head past Saimes' on the way though.' Alissa looked over Shem's shoulder distractedly.

'Okay, well, if you're still there later then we'll see you.' Shem sounded hopeful.

'Sure. Okay.' Alissa walked past him and turned down a corridor. Shem watched her go, but she didn't look back.

She walked alone along the long hallways of the public areas; everything was grey around here, metallic and cold. She wandered around aimlessly, paying no attention to where she was; too busy thinking about life without her friends. She would miss them terribly.

Her life was only tolerable because at the end of a long day she could head out with the guys and have a laugh. They'd head on over to Saime's and drink the cheap alcohol, and laugh and talk. They had all shared the deepest secrets in that place, their friendship had grown and the three of them had become bonded. Now here was the Ark, getting in the way and taking her family away from her.

She swallowed the lump that was forming in her throat. Now she would be alone; she'd have to make more friends, new friends, friends that failed the test too.

She was blinking back the tears as she turned the corner towards the bar; there was no way she could have seen the man before he grabbed her. A shocked squeal had barely escaped her lips before a hand clamped itself over her face and pressed a rag hard into her nostrils, and another arm wrapped around her, pining her arms to her sides. She started feeling dizzy and her eyes were closing. The last thing she saw before her consciousness was taken away was a man with crystal blue eyes.

Alissa opened her eyes and quickly closed them again. There was a bright light above her and it stung her eyes. Her cheek was pressed against a hard, cold concrete floor. She opened her eyes again. The light penetrated right through into her brain till it ached.

She pressed her hands against the ground and pushed herself upright. That's when she realised how hung over she was – her head started pounding and a wave of nausea washed over her. She pressed her hands against her eyes and held her breath for a few seconds but it wasn't enough to stop her stomach contents from escaping through her mouth and her nostrils. Her mind took her back to the night before.

She hadn't even reached the bar; whoever that man was, he'd taken her while she'd been just feet from safety.

Alissa gingerly opened her eyes again and they started adjusting to the harsh light of the room. As she edged away from the mess on the floor she began to take in her surroundings. There really wasn't much to see – four grey walls, concrete floor, little metal table and chair and a sink. Her legs threatened to give way as she stood up, but it was a necessary evil.

Each step was shaky, like a deer learning to walk. She reached the sink and washed her face. It was hot and clammy; whatever they'd done to her had left her weak and sick.

The room boasted a door and as luck would have it there was a good-sized handle right in the middle. If there really was any kind of fortune left in this world she would be able to pull that door open and make good her escape. She walked over and reached her hand to the doorknob. Before her grime smeared hand had a chance to wrap around the metal knob, it started to turn. She jumped back and stood, open-mouthed, as the door swung inwards.

A man stood there, blocking the exit, silhouetted

by the light behind him. Alissa's eyes took in every inch of him. His height was shocking; he could've reached to the ceiling and placed his hand flat against it without even stretching his arm, and he was broad too, his muscles showing through his overalls.

The worst part for Alissa, though, was the mask.

A fresh wave of nausea took her by surprise and she backed away from him towards the wall with her arm out to steady herself. Her eyes closed and she wished she was at home, safe in her own bed. She could hear him walking towards her, slowly, excruciatingly slowly, and her eyes betrayed her and opened again. She tried very hard not to throw up. Looking around for something to defend herself with, she spotted a mysterious red stain on the floor and her fear overcame her. The man was standing in front of her now; she could smell his breath through the mask, and it smelled sour.

'Please, don't hurt me.'

The words were barely audible, her throat felt like it was closing and tears were streaming down her face. The man ignored her pleas and grabbed her by the shoulders. He turned her around so her face was pressed against the wall, disgusting and slimy. He tied her hands behind her back and thrust a bag over her head.

I'm going to die now. This crazy man has kidnapped me and now he's going to kill me.

The man turned her round again and hoisted her effortlessly over his shoulder and started walking. His bony shoulder pressed into her abdomen uncomfortably, and with every step she bounced a little. She held her breath for long periods, praying that she wouldn't throw up again.

After what seemed like an eternity but was probably only a couple of minutes, Alissa was flung unceremoniously to the ground. She lay exactly where she fell, too scared to move. Please just leave this bag on my head; I don't want to see what's coming. She could feel the hot tears pouring down her cheeks but she held back the sobs that should have accompanied them. Footsteps came towards her and a hand grabbed the bag and yanked it free from her head, taking a good chunk of hair with it. She yelped in pain. 'Please, don't kill me,' she said.

'Sit on the chair, Alissa.'

The voice was deep and authoritative. She opened her eyes and saw she was on the floor of a very dark room. She couldn't make out where the walls were so she had no idea how big the room actually was. The only furniture she could make out was a big metal table, on the far side of which were four chairs, each with a man sitting motionless and silent. On the side closest to her was an empty chair.

She walked over to it and sat down. The four men in front of her were frighteningly similar looking. One had the most beautiful blue eyes she had ever seen and she sat, open-mouthed, staring into the endless pools of blue.

He spoke first.

'Alissa Namaah, you have been brought before us because you

have a duty to perform.' She looked at him, confused. 'I don't have any duties. I'm just a mechanic.'

The one sitting next to Blue Eyes had a scar beneath his lip and

Alissa's eyes traced it down his chin as he spoke: 'You have failed the aptitude test; therefore you will remain on Earth until it burns.'

Tears threatened her again. They knew she was a failure; why were they doing this?

'I didn't mean to ...' Her tiny voice trailed off as the man sitting directly across from her, wearing the silver glove, cleared his throat. He had been staring at her intently and finally he spoke. But his voice was gentle and kind.

'Alissa, how could you expect to pass the test when you guessed every single answer?'

'I don't … I don't know.' Her voice kept catching in her throat.

Silver Glove continued.

'We don't want to upset you, Alissa. We want to help you. I know you want to be with your friends when they leave. Am I right?' Alissa nodded while she held back fresh tears. 'And the only way to do that now is to win your place on the lottery. But that has no guarantee. We don't want you trapped here alone. You've done very valuable work on a great many ships. We know you have the knowledge to work on the Ark; the aptitude test was just …' – he paused for a minute; he might have been looking for the right word, or he might have been waiting so the word would have more impact – '…unfair.'

The test was unfair. She knew more than most of the people in there and they managed to pass. She knew she didn't test well but that was no reason to be left behind. She didn't mind admitting she was annoyed at the aptitude test, and she was becoming more interested in what this silver-gloved man had to say. She stared at him intently while he continued.

'We have a job for you. And when it is complete you will be able to walk onto the Ark with your friends and leave this planet far behind you. Isn't that what you want?'

She nodded for the second time.

'So, Miss Namaah, will you work for us?'

She looked at the other three men, who hadn't moved at all during the entire exchange. They were creepy, but she couldn't help liking the man with the glove. He understood her and her fears. If they needed her, and they were willing to free her from the shackles of failure, then she would do whatever she had to.

She slowly nodded her head, and Silver Glove smiled.

***

Ham and Shem sat in Saime's. The bigger man was hungrily eating some stale biscuits out of a bowl while his smaller companion sipped at his drink, his eyes flitting around the bar.

'I don't think she's here.' Ham blew out biscuit crumbs while he spoke.

'I wasn't looking for Alissa.'

'Yeah you were. It's okay though, I get it.'

Shem looked at his friend with obvious scepticism.

'What exactly do you get?'

'You love her.'

Shem had just taken a mouthful of his drink which he spat out when Ham dropped his bombshell.

'I don't love her! I mean ... I do, because she's my friend. But I

don't ... like ... love her. I just love her. You know?'

'It's okay. She's a good person. She takes care of me. I'm glad you love her.'

Shem took a deep breath, ready to challenge his friend's accusation, but what would have been the point?

'When the Hell did you get so perceptive?'

'You think she doesn't love you back?'

'I don't think it would matter if she did. I'm a navigation officer, Ham, and that comes with certain expectations. The guys I work with don't see Alissa, or any of the other mechanics for that matter, as a potential match. They see them as subordinates that are only here to do the dirty work.' Shem stared deeply into his drink because he didn't dare to look at Ham.

'But, she's your friend already.'

'Yeah, she is. And you are too. And they don't really understand it but to take it further would be like occupational suicide. I can't risk it; regardless of any feelings I may or may not have. Okay?'

Ham nodded and stuffed more biscuits into his mouth.

'I gotta get going, Ham. I need to … do some stuff. Okay?'

Ham nodded as Shem drained his glass, stood up and left the bar. Ham finished his own drink and walked over to a door hidden away at the other side of the room. It led to the airlock.

He walked in and the door closed behind him. These tiny rooms were always unpleasant and this particular one was no different. It was grey and had a light dusty layer covering everything. With only two suits hanging on the wall it was not well equipped but it was sufficient for his needs.

He reached out, took one from a peg and began squeezing his ample frame into it. It was halfway up his thighs when he realised it wasn't going to fit, and it was beginning to cut off his circulation. He tugged it off, hung it back up and reached for the other.

He slowly pulled this one on, zipped it up and attached the helmet; it clicked into place with a hiss, letting him know that he now had an air supply. He pressed the button on the external door and waited for a few moments until a high-pitched whine indicated that it was safe to exit, and the external door opened. Ham stepped out and looked around.

It was always dusty outside, and the small particles swirled around him, clouding his vision. He began walking, kicking his feet through the thick, grey powder that covered every inch of his surroundings. He enjoyed his walks because they were nice and peaceful; no one was here to tell him he was stupid or laugh at the way he talked. He thought about Shem. Shem never laughed at him; he was his best friend and he took care of him.

Ham wandered through the old cracked streets of a city now forgotten. His brother used to take him out here when he was a little boy. His parents didn't know, it was their secret adventure and he adored it. They would run through the empty streets, surrounded by crumbing relics of the past, imagining they were detectives or adventurers or the sole survivors of some horrific incident.

He looked up to the sky and thought of his family and missed them terribly. But his brother was safe. Since he was offered passage on the Ark six years ago, he had been helping to establish New World, and Ham would soon be there – now that he had passed the test. But how will I work on the ship, he thought. I have to take the drugs with me. He knew Alissa and Shem would disapprove, but they were his best friends, his amily in fact. They would understand. And when I get to New World, I'll stop. But part of him knew that he wouldn't be able to. He liked himself when he was taking them, he liked being smart.

He looked around the old landscape. He could make out the tall buildings that surrounded him and he wondered what Earth was like before the Incident. He tried to picture the area he was in, tried to imagine himself surrounded by people, living their lives, going to work, going shopping, having parties with little buffets and posh drinks; he could think of it all but couldn't truly picture any of it. His imagination wasn't that good anymore. When he was little he used to imagine all sorts of games that he could play by himself or with his brother, but since he started taking the drugs he'd struggled with a lot of things.

He leant against a dusty wall and frowned. How had he become a stupid druggie? He slid down to the ground and started flicking bits of rock across the street. Maybe I should try talking to Alissa. She always understood him and she never shouted at him. He smiled as he thought of her; she took good care of him. He tried to flick another bit of rock but instead his gloved finger struck against something that wasn't moving. He looked down and started moving away the dust. He didn't quite understand what he was looking at but he knew it wasn't normal, it wasn't right. It was a panel with buttons and lights, attached to some kind of sealed hatchway. He knew there would be something important down there and he wanted to know what – one thing he had never lost was his passion for adventure. He stood up and looked around to get his bearings. He wanted to make sure he would be able to find this place again. Then he turned and headed back to the airlock.

CHAPTER SEVEN

SHEM STARED AT THE LETTER. THIS MUST BE A joke. it was from the captain, congratulating him on the highest score his department had ever seen. His legs betrayed him and he sat down on his bed, still staring at the letter. His bedroom was small and crammed full of gadgets and gizmos. He'd lived there for years now, ever since he moved to the complex with Ham, and in that time he had collected hundreds of little trinkets, things he could study and program. His room was bland and spare, cream carpet matching cream walls.

He read the letter again, more slowly. It was inviting him to a luncheon with the captain to discuss his promotion within the department. His face broke into a smile and he finally allowed himself to believe it. He leapt from his bed and ran out the door, down the hallway into his living space. There was nothing bland about this area. He had painted it turquoise because he liked the colour, thought it was bright and interesting; it cheered him up when he was alone in his tiny quarters.

He almost took a tumble as he went past his terminal, but he managed to right himself, and stabbed at the panel frantically. Ham's terminal relayed the message that he wasn't home right now so Shem, now slightly frustrated, keyed in Alissa's call code. Her terminal had been turned off and all Shem got was the loud beeps. His face darkened, partly with concern for their whereabouts but also with selfish anger that they weren't there to share his news. He walked across the living room and crashed onto his couch. This was the biggest thing that had ever happened to him and his best friends where nowhere to be found.

He got up and paced the floor for a few minutes, thinking about his deserting friends. When the terminal rang his face lit up. At least one of them had gotten back to him – he knew they hadn't abandoned him. He crossed the room in two strides, stopped in front of the screen and pressed answer. A wide smile began to spread across his handsome features, making them friendlier, more open, but it ceased abruptly when an unknown face popped up on the screen.

'Shem?' The face was long and thin and the voice was scratchy.

'Yes, that's me. Who are you?'

'My name is Vincent. Are you free to talk my friend?'

'Uh … yeah. Sure.' Shem's eyes narrowed as he looked at the man with greasy hair. Vincent, on the other hand, looked quite at ease with the whole conversation.

'Good. I was told you were most knowledgeable about quantum
mechanics.'

Shem relaxed slightly. There was no one better at QM, that's why he was promoted before Shelby, who had been hounding him for a year about being inferior.

'I am.'

'That's excellent! Meet me in Saime's Bar in twenty minutes; we have a lot to discuss.'

'For example?'

'Well, how about the algorithms, and the assumptions they're based on – that would be a start?'

Shem thought about this for a moment. The last paper he'd written was on just that subject. A coincidence? Or was this man up to something?

'I'll be there.' Shem turned off the screen and frowned. He'd just agreed to meet a very strange-looking man in a quiet little bar. He wasn't suspicious by nature but the man made him feel uneasy. On the other hand, there was a massive promotion on the cards and no one to celebrate with, so he was going to grab this night with both hands and enjoy it no matter what. He wandered to the shower room. If he was hitting a bar tonight then he was going to do it in style. Business then pleasure, he thought.

He turned on the shower and held his hand under the trickle of water. The pressure was pathetic in staff quarters, but then most things were pretty awful in the little tin boxes they called living quarters. He sat on the toilet and waited for the water to heat up and looked around the little wet room. Grey tiles covered the floor, walls and ceiling. He kept meaning to replace them with something a little more...turquoise, but never got round to it.

Steam began to rise from the shower area indicating that the water was good and hot, ready to cleanse him of his daily work and replace the scummy Shem with a cleaner, better-looking version.

He removed his clothes and stepped under the shower head. He was permanently engrained with dirt and he didn't quite know why – he didn't have a particularly dirty job. One of the perils, perhaps, of living in a complex. He squirted shampoo onto his hair and began massaging his scalp. His imagination produced a likeness of the letter and his mind's eye read it greedily, eating up each glowing recommendation and every transparent compliment, ignoring the pretentiousness of it all. *I'm really gonna be someone now, someone important.* He looked forward to his dinner with the captain; it was going to be an honour to meet him, shake his hand, and break bread with him.

He rinsed his hair, turned the shower off and gave himself a little shake before hopping out and walking over to the sink to shave. Maybe I'll meet a nice girl, one that actually answers my calls. He was surprised by his thought; it invaded his peace and reminded him that he was alone, without Alissa. He shook his head to get rid of it, and brushed his teeth.

After inspecting his naked reflection, and concluding that it was pretty decent, he returned to his room, pulled out his favourite clean shirt and a pair of pants and got dressed. He gave himself a quick spritz of cologne and exchanged another smile with his reflection. Not bad, he thought, not bad at all. He walked with purpose down the hall and through the living space to the front door, stepped outside and headed towards the bar.

***

Alissa sat on a chair, alone and in semi-darkness. She was staring at her feet, lost in her thoughts. Swirling, confusing images of Ham and Shem danced around in her mind. They must be worried about her by now; surely they must've noticed that she was missing.

'I bet they're going crazy trying to find me.'

Her voice echoed in the dark expanse of the room. The sound made her laugh; she could be her own companion. She had no use for friends now, although they would feel pretty silly when she went back to work.

She thought about the Ark too. It was a ticket to freedom, to the New World, to safety. No one ever said much about the New World but she knew that everyone thought about it. She wondered how long it would take to get there.

'Can't be that long.' She was thinking out loud more often now, mainly because it was nice to hear a voice, even her own. She hadn't seen the four men for a while now and she didn't know exactly how long it had been since anyone spoke to her. The strange thing was, she didn't feel hungry, or tired, she just felt content, like the air alone was enough to keep her alive. Absurd, of course, she thought. The human body needs sustenance to survive. How long had it been since she had eaten?

She heard a sound coming from outside the room and her eyes widened; she hadn't heard anything except her own voice since she had been left there. She lifted her head and strained to make out shapes in the darkness. Unable to tell where exactly the door was, she gazed in the general direction of the noise. Despite the darkness, she wasn't afraid, and for a reason she couldn't explain there was a constant thought in the back of her mind: The man in the silver glove will keep me safe …

The door slowly opened to reveal a silhouette against the brightness beyond. A shaft of light filled the room, and as Alissa's eyes adjusted she took in her surroundings. Not much, she thought: four concrete walls and a door.

The silhouette entered the room and she could see him clearly now. It was the man in the silver glove. He stood, casting his shadow over her, in a stylish black suit which looked strangely out of place in this dank and featureless room.

He smiled as he walked towards her and she felt her stomach flip; there was something about his unquestionably handsome face that made her ache for him. He knelt on the floor in front of her chair and looked at her for a while, his dark eyes searching every inch of her, learning about her. She in turn looked at him, watching as a lock of thick hair fell onto his forehead in just the right way. He had full, almost feminine lips and a sweet smile. He was tall and she could see his muscles bulge through his suit.

She slid down off the chair and sat on the floor in front of him.

'I'm sorry it's been so long.' Even his voice was beautiful.

'It's okay. I don't mind.' Alissa stared at him. He was perfect.

'I came to tell you ...'' He paused. 'You're not ready yet.'

'You mean I have to stay here?' She looked at the floor and fought fiercely to hold back the tears.

'You don't have to stay much longer. But the task we have set will be hard for you. We need to know you are ready. If you don't trust me – with everything you have – then you will fail. And if you fail, they will kill you.'

He rested his hand on hers. She sighed deeply and nodded her head.

'I understand.'

'Good,' he smiled. ''I have something for you to eat, you must be starving.'

As he stood up and walked to the doorway she realised just how hungry she actually was. How long had it been since she had eaten? Hours, maybe even days – it was impossible to tell in here. She touched a hand to her stomach, which was beginning to cramp with hunger pains. Silver Glove returned carrying a tray. He placed it onto the floor, stood up straight and looked at her.

'Make sure you eat it all,' he said in his silken voice, before turning round walking out of the room.

Alissa scrambled over to the tray like a half-starved animal. Her hands pulled at the covering and she tossed is aside as her eyes locked onto the food. There was the freshest fruit, the purest water, the juiciest meat and crunchiest-looking vegetables she'd ever seen, all beautifully laid out for her to enjoy. Food like this had never crossed her path before and it made her smile; she wanted to savour every bite, but the growling coming from her midsection was demanding otherwise.

Her fingers played along the edge of the tray and eagerly picked up a plump red berry; she'd seen it in pictures but never in the flesh.

'Strawberry,' she whispered. She couldn't remember ever speaking the word aloud before. There was no reason to – you didn't get this sort of food in the complex. Her first thought was that it couldn't possibly be real. She popped it into her mouth and chewed. The flavour exploded across her tongue and her eyes widened. The sweet juice danced around her taste buds. It was almost too much to take.

She reached out and ate another; then, as though possessed, she began jamming food into her mouth in handfuls, mixing the flavours and enjoying every second. She was baffled as to how food like this even existed in the complex, but she wasn't asking any questions. The whole plate vanished in minutes and she cursed herself for not savouring it more, but it was evident that when it came to real, fresh food her willpower was less than impressive.

Surprisingly, the glass of water survived longer than anything else. Her hands wrapped around the plastic beaker and she gently lifted it to her lips. As she tilted it back the water flowed down her throat, a refreshing, ice-cold torrent of pure nectar.

She pushed the tray away and lay on the concrete floor. Her eyelids felt heavy and she struggled to stay awake. Eventually she gave in and with a satisfied sigh, she fell into a deep sleep.

CHAPTER EIGHT

HAM WALKED INTO HIS APARTMENT. IT WAS BRIGHT and garish. Huge light bulbs scared away anything that might have resembled a shadow. Nothing could hide in the dark in Ham's house. Ham really liked things to be bright and safe.

His living space had yellow walls which had obviously been painted by an amateur hand, and a rough red carpet with jagged edges clashed terribly with the green furniture that was dotted around. That was Ham all over; no thought for the big picture and all choices according to whatever he liked best at the time. It was a charming little annoyance that bothered no one after their second or third visit.

He crossed the living room and walked into his bedroom. A very regal blue. In the corner, a large canopy bed, savagely thrown together by his hard hand from scrap he had found in the garage. As haphazard as it was, to Ham it looked delicate and special. He loved his bed.

Facing the door was an antique set of drawers he had acquired from his elderly neighbour after she had passed away.

On top of the drawers were beautifully framed pictures. By his own admission, Ham was a sentimental man; the photographs were mostly of himself with Shem and Alissa but there were a few from his childhood. He was always pictured with the same boy when he was a child; a very similar looking boy, but older and skinnier. His brother was his best friend throughout his younger years and taught him all the best games.

On the wall above the drawers was a large mirror. It was wooden but painted silver, with wonderfully ornate and intricate carving around the edge. It didn't seem to fit with the room, but that was because it had been passed from his mother to his brother, and then to him. He didn't dare paint it a brighter colour in case his brother wanted it back when Ham got to the New World.

He walked over to his shelves and picked up a little box. He sat down on the edge of the bed, opening the box to reveal dozens of little packets made of cheap brown paper.

He plucked one out, and with it a little tube. Closing the lid, he placed the box beside him on the bed.

He carefully tore the top of the packet off and looked inside at the dark green powder. He had never gotten used to the smell. Ham picked up the little tube and slipped one end into the packet and the other deep into his nostril. He snorted long and hard, then checked that the little packet was empty.

His face felt like it was on fire. Through watery eyes Ham watched the box tumble off the bed as he jerked and twisted. He hated this – why did he do it to himself? He had to stop. He dropped the packet and tube on the floor. He grabbed his nose and started rubbing it. He pressed his hands against his eyes for a few minutes until the pain started to fade and the fog that had wrapped its long, misty fingers round his brain began to clear.

He blinked hard a couple of times and looked around the room. It was different now. It didn't feel comfortable to him anymore; it felt childish and wrong.

He bent down, picked up the tube and the empty packet. Turning it around in his fingers he began to think about his habit. Was it really that big of a problem? It didn't affect him on a personal level. He still loved his friends fiercely, and if anything he understood the emotion better.

He took a few more packets from the little box and caught his reflection in the mirror. His hair was a mess and a little trickle of blood was making its way from his nose to his top lip. Frowning, he wiped at his nose, cleaning away the little red streak. He took a brush out of the drawer and made an attempt to neaten his hair but after a few minutes he gave up, tossed the brush onto the bed and walked out of the room.

His brain was beginning to pick up speed now. The first few minutes were always the longest; everything seemed to slow down, but things were becoming clearer now. He thought about his reasons for taking the drug and knew where he had to go now. He walked out of his front door and headed down the corridor to the airlock.

**

Shem strolled into Saime's Bar. As usual it was sticky-floored and dank. He looked around and caught sight of the greasy man that had called. Vincent was sitting alone at a corner table, almost hidden from view. Shem wondered why the man would seclude himself so drastically when meeting someone for the first time. It made him uneasy.

He made his way over to the table and seated himself across from Vincent. The metal table was marked with stains and rings; each told a story of a night forgotten by the drunk who'd left it there. Vincent looked at Shem and motioned to the barman; there was an empty pitcher on the table and he looked pointedly into its hollowness.

They sat in silence for a few moments, and as the seconds ticked by Shem became more uncomfortable. He wanted to say something but couldn't find the words. After what seemed like an eternity, Vincent seemed to think it was time to talk.

'Shem, it's a pleasure to meet you.'

Before Shem could respond the barman walked over with a pitcher of carbonated alcohol and a couple of empty glasses, and half-dropped them onto the table. The service here wasn't great but the beer was cheap and that was enough to keep the bar full of patrons. Vincent poured the drinks with slow deliberation and Shem watched. Vincent handed him one of the glasses and kept one for himself. When they each took a mouthful Shem flinched at the bitter taste, but his greasy companion seemed to enjoy it.

They got through two more pitchers in a short space of time, and the uneasiness between them began to fade into real camaraderie until both men were behaving like the best of friends. Shem lifted his grimy glass to his lips and drained the last drops, and as he went to put it back on the table, it slipped, falling from his grasp and smashing into a thousand tiny pieces as it hit the floor. Shem began to laugh. He was drunk. Vincent, on the other hand, was curiously sober.

'Shem, I like you, you're a great character.' Vincent's words were dripping with condescension, but Shem was way too drunk to notice.

'Aw, thanks man!' Shem smiled at his new friend. 'Hey, are you
gonna be on the Ark? We should get together again if you are!'

Vincent kept very cool at this point. This was what he was waiting for. This was his moment. He was going to need to use every sales technique in the book to pull this off.

'Unfortunately my expertise wasn't gained until after I failed the aptitude test. I'm more than capable of running a star ship engine entirely by myself. Ah well ... I'm older now and somewhat redundant in the grand scheme of things. I do wish it was different though. Can you imagine what it's like, knowing that you will have to spend the rest of your life on this planet with no hope of escape?'

''I ... uh ... no. I can't.' Shem frowned. 'I'm sorry. To have the knowledge that you do and not be able to use it must really suck.' He was slurring his words now.

'Add to that the fact that this planet may not have much longer left...' Vincent's voice caught in his throat. A very convincing performance, he thought to himself. He rested his head in his hands.

'What am I going to do?'

Shem looked like a light bulb had switched on inside his head. 'Join my team!'

'What?' Vincent raised his head to look at Shem. 'Your team?'

'Yeah! I was promoted – or I will be. I get to put my own team together! If you know as much as you say you do, you'd be perfect.' Shem smiled at Vincent, who was now shamelessly allowing the tears to fall. You are so good, he thought to himself.

'Thank you Shem! You have saved my life.'

'It'll be a pleasure to work with you.' Shem rose to his feet and waved at the barman. 'Another round over here, Barkeep!'

The fat, sweaty barman wandered over to their table and plonked another jug of fizzy alcohol in front of them. Now they were drinking as a team. Now they were friends. Vincent raised his glass.

'To the newest member of the Ark Crew … me!'

Shem smiled. This guy isn't too bad. Maybe I don't need Alissa and Ham so much. I can make new friends.

'What are you thinking about buddy?'

'I was just … moving on from the past.'

'Good, we have a promising future ahead of us my friend.'

'I think we should head out of here.'

Vincent raised an eyebrow. ''Where do you propose we go?'

'To The Zone. Of course.' Shem smiled. The Zone was a nightclub for the workers. It was dark and dingy and it smelled bad but the alcohol was cheap, the music was loud and the women were usually both.

The Zone was a tunnel-walk away from Saimes'. It wasn't a safe journey but it was one that hundreds of workers travelled every week. To survive a tunnel-walk you had to go with as many people as you could. Usually people loitered in the entrances waiting for others to turn up who would walk with them. You could wait for a couple of hours before anyone did but the risk of doing it alone was too much for most people. And the ones that were brave enough didn't usually make it out the other end.

The walkways were filled with The Unpleasant Ones – people from the small towns. They had no money, jobs or food and they would kill you if they outnumbered you. It was said that they were cannibals, but there was no evidence to prove that. They hid in the tunnels to escape the gasses. Occasionally city guards with armoured carts would come and move them along, back out into the wilds of the towns, but they always came back.

Shem and Vincent arrived at the tunnel door and saw a few people waiting, a young woman on her own and two smartly dressed men. There was only one reason to take this tunnel and that was The Zone. Shem, in his drunken state, concluded that the people waiting there must be heading their way. Five people would be enough to make the journey, he reckoned. The businessmen must've thought the same thing because they started walking towards them.

'Hi, friend!'

Both men were tall and dressed in suits; the blond one seemed friendlier than the balding one.

'Hi.' Shem smiled and looked over at the woman. 'Shall we escort this pretty lady through the tunnel?'

The woman walked over to the four men. 'I'd really appreciate that.'

'Not a problem.' Shem held out his arm and the woman linked her own through it. The little group of five of started towards the doorway.

The tunnel was dimly lit and smelled bad – urine mixed with rotten food. At least, Shem hoped it was food. The alternative was bodies in the shadows. He shook his head to rid himself of such visions.

The five new friends walked along holding each other; it was safer if they all kept physical contact at all times. This particular tunnel was only a mile long but it was one of the worst. They were about halfway through when a crash echoed all around them. The source was hard to judge but it was close – loud enough to ring in Shem's ears. The halls were usually silent, so something that loud was enough to send warning signals. The group froze, worried what might come next.

They were barely breathing and the young lady was shaking with fear.

'I knew I shouldn't have come here,' she whispered.

Shem wrapped his arm protectively around her. It had been a long time since his arm had been around a woman. Even in such a terrifying situation, he took the time to breathe her in. Her hair smelled like flowers, which was a welcome distraction from the stench of their surroundings.

They heard footsteps, and they were getting closer. Shem's consciousness was dragged back to reality, away from the

mental meadow he'd found himself frolicking in. The businessmen were looking around frantically. The blond one pointed at the wall and the two of them rushed over, returning with one large wooden post apiece. They stood there holding their posts up high, like hitters looking for a line drive.

The footsteps were getting closer still. The girl spun round to face Shem; she flung her arms round his neck and buried her face in his chest. Any other time, thought Shem.

Stadler reached into his jacket, took out a small pistol and held it in his shaking hand.

The footsteps stopped.

Three men walked out of the shadows and headed towards the frightened group. The bald man screamed and ran towards the Unpleasant Ones with the wooden post held high. He hit the first one clean in the head and everyone stopped for a moment as he fell to the ground, his skull caved in. If the bald man hadn't hesitated, if he hadn't thought about what he'd just done, what happened next might have been avoided. In a moment of panic or maybe even guilt, he dropped the post. Shem thought, just for a second, that he must have had a death wish. Maybe he'd given up. Taking a life, even that of an Unpleasant One, was something you couldn't come back from.

The remaining two Unpleasant Ones dragged the man to the ground and set about tearing him to pieces with their bare hands. The others looked on in horror. The blond businessman dropped his post too. It seemed he was too afraid to use it. They stood in silence and watched as the balding man was killed. His final moments were filled with agony and his screams tore through the air. Then everything went quiet. The two attackers, now covered in fresh blood, rose to their feet and turned to face their next victims. Stadler took a step forward and with a shaking hand, fired two shots. One was hit in the eye and went down as the hollow-tip bullet exploded in his head, a look of open-mouthed surprise momentarily registering on his scarred and filthy face.

The other took the bullet to the chest. It slowed him but he wasn't down yet. He began charging towards Stadler, wild-eyed and bloodied, but Stadler pulled the trigger a third time and the man fell to the ground, blood pumping freely from his neck and forming a pool on the packed earth of the tunnel floor. The woman started weeping as Shem held her.

'Come on, let's go. We're nearly through.' He motioned forwards into the darkness and they started moving slowly. The blond man didn't look as they walked past the remains of his friend. His eyes were focused on something in the distance. They increased their speed and reached the other end of the tunnel in record time. As the complex door closed and locked behind them, each of them breathed a sigh of relief, glad to be alive. Stadler leaned forward and put his hands on his knees, gasping – as much from shock as exhaustion. The blond man, without saying a word, turned and walked towards the club. He clearly wanted to leave the group, and no one protested. His first thought would no doubt be to drink away the horror, then he'd probably advise the security patrols so that anything that was left of the bald man could be retrieved for a proper burial.

The woman, on the other hand, was still clinging onto Shem. She had never seen anything like that before and while everyone knew the stories it was a different thing entirely to witness it. The sounds of the man's screams would stay with her forever. She vowed to herself never to return to The Zone.

Vincent was confident now. He'd killed two UOs and that was a badge of honour in the circles he moved in. He'd never had the opportunity to do his duty before and it felt really good. All citizens were expected to cleanse the complexes of UOs. It was instilled in everyone from birth. They weren't like real people. They were subhuman cannibals and they deserved to die.

He was eagerly anticipating his hero's welcome in the club, once people knew how close he came to death, how he'd singlehandedly slaughtered those fiends, how he'd tried to save the bald man but just wasn't quick enough. He'd already embellished most of the details and would be on free drinks all night.

The three of them walked up to the entrance of The Zone and two of them paid the fee. Vincent talked his way in for free. He headed to the bar while Shem looked at the woman by his side. She was quite pretty with long brown hair and blue eyes. She was shorter than him, that was good, and she had a nice curvy body.

'I'm thirsty.' Her voice interrupted his assessment. She wants a drink. He turned towards the bar and shouted over his shoulder, "Get us a table!" He walked to the bar and stood beside Stadler.

'She's a pretty little thing isn't she?' True to form.

Shem looked over at her. 'Yeah, she's nice.'

'Allow me to excuse myself then, my friend. There are people here I know and I wouldn't want to play third wheel.'

'Oh.' Shem realised what Vincent was saying. 'It's not like that. She's nice and all but … I don't know …' Shem stared at her. From this distance, in this low light, she looked like someone else.

'Listen, you're young, free and you've just got the promotion of your dreams. Take a bottle of the classy stuff, two glasses and treat her like a lady. Get it?' Vincent waved over to the barman as he spoke.

'Barkeep, a bottle of your finest wine for my friend here.'

'And two glasses, said Shem, smiling as the barman turned away to get the drink. 'You're right Vincent. I'm going to enjoy my night.'

The barman placed a bottle of what might have been wine in another age, and two passably clean glasses, in front of the men. Shem reached into his pocket and Vincent stopped him.

'No Shem, allow me.'

He pulled some cash out of his wallet and handed it to the barman, who waved it away.

'The hero's money is no good here,' he said.

Vincent smiled his slimy smile as he turned and walked away. My friend the hero, thought Shem, as he grabbed the bottle and glasses and headed over to the table.

He put the bottle down and handed the girl a glass. She smiled at him as he poured her a drink, a crooked smile which was kind of pretty, though he had a thing for symmetry. As he sat down she slid right up beside him.

'Tell me your name,' she purred. Her earlier terror had been replaced with desire – desire for drink, maybe for Shem. She wanted desperately to forget what had happened and he was the perfect opportunity.

'Shem Mitchell. And who might you be?'

'Sophia.' She smiled.

Crooked.

'I'm glad you were there tonight,' she went on. 'I wouldn't have

wanted to hold anyone else that close.' She smiled seductively at Shem. This girl, he thought, clearly wanted only one thing. 'Let's finish this bottle and head back with one of the big groups; there's one leaving in half an hour and I have something I want to show you.'

Two hours later they were drunkenly staggering out of the club. One bottle had turned into three and now they were headed to the group area; this was a popular spot for folks to meet up to travel through the tunnel. It happened more often as the night wore on. By the early hours of the morning you could travel through a tunnel and barely notice where you were. The UOs knew better than to attack such a large group.

There were at least eleven people there already, and with Shem and Sophia they had enough people to make the journey without seeing a single UO. As they walked Shem watched for the bald man's remains but there was nothing left at the spot where they lost him. He was appalled by the implications, and sincerely hoped that one of the patrols had found the body first.

When they emerged, Shem took Sophia by the hand and led her to his apartment. When they reached the door and she leant against it and pulled him towards her. They kissed passionately and she pulled his body closer. This girl wants me. Shem wrapped one arm around her and used the other to open the door. He pulled her inside and guided her to the bedroom. They fell onto the bed and began pulling at each other's clothes.

***

In the dusty cityscape, Ham knelt on the ground beside a large metal panel. He'd taken too long to find this place again; maybe his mind wasn't as sharp as usual. But he was here now and that was what mattered.

He pulled out a long thin tool and clicked it into a small slot in the control pad. After a few moments of silent work the lid on the control panel clicked open. Ham's sturdy, practiced hands played with the wires, then suddenly there was a loud pop and a flash of sparks. He dropped the wires and heard a loud whirring noise followed by an alarm. Nothing too loud, just a warning that the hatch was opening.

This is it, he thought. Something that no one has seen in years. Ham excitedly lowered his ample frame down through the hatch and dropped into the room below. It was a perfectly square room. Perfectly square and completely empty. The walls were bare and the floor was cold steel. He turned in a small circle. There was only a door, the same steel as the floor. He stared intently at the door; he would do anything to know where it would lead him. Would he open it to be faced with a hundred enemies? Unlikely, but not impossible. After some deliberation he reasoned that anyone down there would have heard the hatch alarm and come to investigate. He was probably safe.

The door gently swung open when he pushed it, revealing a marginally bigger room which, with its little desk and its metal chairs, looked remarkably like an office. There was a map printed on the wall, and one of the rooms on the map was blue. That must be the 'you are here' part, Ham thought as he looked at it. There was another door, and according to the map it would lead to a tunnel. Ham walked to the door and took a deep breath, preparing himself.

CHAPTER NINE

'I NEED YOU TO OPEN YOUR EYES NOW ALISSA. AND I need you to focus.'

Silver Glove had woken her from her slumbers. It had been happening like this again and again. She didn't know how much time had passed but she supposed it didn't matter.

Silver Glove would wake her up, ask how she felt, what she was thinking; give her food – and leave. She would realise that she was starving and she would stuff the food down her throat and fall into a deep asleep.

This time was different, though. Silver Glove was standing beside her sparse and flimsy bed looking over her. She felt suddenly exposed. She was wearing the same clothes she had been taken in, but that didn't stop her feeling like her privacy was invaded.

'Come with me.' A gloved hand reached out to her and she took it in her own. Suddenly she was on her feet looking into his face. He was beautiful, there was no doubt about that, but it was an uncommon beauty. In her eyes he was ... art. Then he smiled and her heart melted.

His grip tightened and he led her out of the room. They stepped out into an ornate corridor with carved wooden doors on either side. It stretched away in both directions as far as she could see. They turned left, walked a few steps down the corridor and stopped in front of a door. It was identical to all the others and Alissa couldn't help wondering how he managed to separate each one in his mind – she never would.

'In here, Alissa.'

He opened the door and they walked in. This room was better than the last one she was in, but only just. Low budget, she thought, looking around. It reminded her of an old school room, with a single steel framed desk in the middle, and a tubular steel chair with moulded plywood seat. It faced a wall with a large screen embedded into it, framed by hundreds of tiny buttons, probably, she thought, designed to show dozens of videos.

'OK Alissa, take a seat.'

She walked to the little metal chair, turned it sideways, and sat down. Silver Glove walked over to the screen and turned it on. The screen started off a bright blue then flicked to an image of the Ark.

'Alissa, you've been chosen. You're the only one who can help us. The mission you're being charged with is not a pleasant one but the sooner it's done, the sooner you can go back to your life and your friends. You understand that, right?'

Alissa nodded but he just stared at her. She stared right back at him, not knowing what he wanted from her. His eyes flickered over to a small microphone on the wall beside the door. This is all recorded.

They need a record of what happens in here.

'Of course I do,' she said. She didn't.

'Good. There is a man, Alissa. And he is not a good man.' Silver
Glove walked over to a cabinet and leant casually against its wooden frame. 'He is going to sabotage the Ark mission.'

Alissa shifted uncomfortably in her seat and frowned. 'Who would want to sabotage the Ark?'

'You're not going to want to believe this, Alissa.'

He pressed a couple of buttons beside the screen and a picture of a man appeared. A recognisable man, a man whose face she knew well. Alissa's eyes widened. 'Captain Andover! You can't mean him. Why would he sabotage his own ship?'

Alissa stared at the screen, confused and more than a little upset.

'Listen to me Alissa, that man is not what he seems. He was sent here to prevent the survival of the human race.' He was pacing in front of the screen. 'Please believe me. Millions of lives are at stake. Every other Ark that has left this planet has been destroyed. No one has survived. It's taken us ten years to find this out and now that we know, we're not going to let it happen again. Clarke Andover cannot be allowed to destroy the Ark. It's our last chance to save the human race.' Alissa was already questioning what she knew.

'I don't understand. In two years there will be another Ark!'

'No, there won't. This planet is not going to last another two years. This is it, Alissa, it's now. The fate of all humanity rests on your shoulders. I know you're strong enough to fight. That's why I chose you. I chose you.' He picked up a glass of water and some fruit from the cabinet, and placed them in front of her. Alissa realised she was starving. She began to eat and, as usual, it tasted wonderful.

She knew now that she would do whatever he asked of her. If the captain was going to destroy the Ark then she would stop him.

'What do you say to all this Alissa?' He rested his hand on hers.

'I'll kill him, whatever it takes.' I'll kill him. The words felt alien on her tongue. She'd never uttered that phrase and meant it as much as she did now. She felt sick.

'Good. Now follow me.'

Silver Glove led her out of the room and they followed the corridor for a while. They walked in complete silence, her hand in his. She'd never had someone hold her hand before. It felt strange, but she liked it. He made her feel safe; he would protect her from the others. Which must be why he's here.

They reached a blue door. It was the only door that looked different; it was even her favourite shade, a grey blue that reminded her of the ocean. Silver Glove opened it slowly and stepped inside; Alissa followed him in and gasped. The room was lined from floor to ceiling with a dull metal and there was some kind of structure in the middle; she tightened her grip.

It was cold in here and she could see her breath. There were computer panels sunk into every wall and monitors surrounding the equipment. She took a step backwards, instinctively wanting to run.

'By now Alissa, you should trust me. No harm will come to you in this room.'

LIAR ... She felt the panic rising.

'This is a safe place.' He glanced down. The knuckles of her hand were white where she gripped his. He walked her over to the central structure. He placed her hand on the cold steel; his hand fell out of hers as she stroked the steel rail in front of her.

'Here is where you will learn to fight. This machine will create the assassin you will need to be to kill the captain. Please, sit.'

If she had known more about science and the human body she probably would've realised that this was going to be a very painful, unpleasant experience. She looked at the structure and realised that in the midst of a jumble of wires and terminals was a metal seat. She stepped through a gap in the rail and worked her way towards it, dodging cables and screens. Her face turned back to Silver Glove, who nodded encouragement. Turning back to the seat she took a deep breath. Pushing her fears aside, she sat down on it and rested her feet on the foot rest.

Silver Glove had followed her, and as she seated herself he lowered a piece of machinery suspended on steel cables, and placed it on her head like a helmet. He pulled some kind of hinged screen over her eyes. 'Relax now Alissa. This will be a necessary evil.'

With the helmet on she was completely blinded to the outside world and within seconds the sensory deprivation was causing her imagination to go wild. She heard beeps and tapping noises – in her head it was the sound of a machine being prepared for her destruction. Don't be such a baby, she commanded herself. It was pathetic, really, that in her entire life she had never had to fight for anything. She just accepted her lot in life and carried on. She was so weak.

Then suddenly the machine whirred into life and it felt like it was digging into her mind, like it could tell what would affect her the most. She thought about her father and she was presented with graphic images of children beside their parents' corpses, violent images with broken bodies and pain in everyone's eyes. She tried to focus on something else. She thought about her little room – she was safe in there – but the machine showed her the devastating aftermath of explosions, people still in their beds, burned to a crisp. She called out for it to stop; she couldn't think anymore, the machine had taken over.

It was showing her graphic and horrifying images beyond her imagining. She shut her eyes, squeezed them closed with all her will but the pictures were in her brain, there was no escaping what they wanted her to see. She clamped her hands onto the metal arm rests and screamed. She screamed while tears poured from her eyes, she screamed while her fingers turned white, she screamed while the man in the silver glove watched.

It felt like hours had passed when the helmet was finally removed. Corpses and monsters danced in front of her eyes when she opened them. Exhaustion crippled her and she felt helpless. This is what they're doing to me, and I can't stop it. She cried softly as restraints were removed. She hadn't even noticed them being put on, but she had struggled so hard that at one point she almost flung herself out of the chair.

She wanted to scream again, and run. Run to Shem – he would hold her and stroke her hair. He would make it all better.

'Alissa?'

'Shem?' Alissa's eyes flew open. Could it all have been in her head? Was Shem here now waking her up? Am I late for my shift?

Her surroundings came into focus and with them, the cables and monitors. Her heart sank and in the midst of it was that exquisite face, smiling at her with a radiantly beautiful smile. He was wearing a silver glove.

'I know that was hard for you. But we have to desensitise you to the emotional stresses that come with death. You have to be cold. You have to be a killer.'

'I can't, it's too much ...' Her voice trailed off.

The silver hand prised her fingers away from the chair and held them gently. He helped her off the chair and let her lean on him as they walked to the door.

'You must go back to your room now and rest.'

Alissa nodded and allowed him to guide her back to her little room, with her little chair, and her little table. He opened the door and she stepped inside. She had barely opened her eyes the whole way back and hadn't even noticed that they had come to another room. It smelled different – that's what gave it away. If it had smelled the same she would've fallen onto the bed and slept.

He encouraged her to open her eyes and that's when she realised the furniture that had sparsely decorated her room was gone. She looked around, absorbed her new surroundings. There was a large, plump looking bed against one wall, covered by a thick duvet. A wooden table with a pretty little tablecloth and matching chair were against another wall and a lamp stood on an end table in the corner. It looked cosy.

Alissa stepped away from the smiling Silver Glove and slowly made her way further into the room. She brushed her fingers along the tablecloth, switched the lamp off and on again. It was delightful. She heard a click and turned to thank her captor, but the door was already closed and locked.

Getting horizontal was the only thing on her mind. The bed was as comfy as it looked, and as she pulled the covers around herself a deep sigh escaped her lips. She wondered what Ham and Shem were doing. Were they worried? Or had the four men taken care of that? Had they told her friends about her mission? They'd probably told them that she'd be home soon. Her mind played on thoughts of Shem, his sweet sandy hair that played in his eyes, his green eyes that were framed by dark eyelashes. She smiled to herself. These were her happiest thoughts.

He always laughed when she was her usual clumsy self. Not laughing at her though, laughing instead at the thought of her. She knew that he loved the thought of her, although he never said as much. His protectiveness balanced her naivety and her innocence. But once the men in suits were finished with her, she wouldn't be so innocent, she wouldn't need protecting. Would he still be there for her? Or would he look at her with disgust?

Would he forgive her if she became a killer?

CHAPTER TEN

ALISSA SMELLED SOMETHING GOOD, SOMETHING buttery and heavy. It permeated her dreams and her eyes flickered open. It was only then that she realised she'd fallen asleep. In only her underwear, she stretched her arms out and rolled herself right up into her duvet. Her body wasn't ready to wake up yet, but her conscious mind was being plagued by images from the day before.

She took a deep breath and kicked off the covers that were keeping her so warm. Her feet shuffled off the side of the bed and onto the floor – the carpeted floor she realised – and dug her toes into the thick shag pile.

She climbed out of bed and looked at the table. The red and white gingham tablecloth was still draped over it from the night before, but now there was an earthenware bowl of warm, freshly baked croissants, a glass of orange juice and a mug full of steaming, black coffee. She almost skipped across the room and sat down on the little wooden chair that sat sideways on to the table. Everything about this was perfect.

The smell was overwhelming and she grabbed one of the pastries and took a huge bite, then paused to savour the moment. She allowed the butter to swirl around her tongue as the soft flakes of croissant fell from her lips. She swallowed, dipped it into her coffee and took another bite.

A few moments later, she leant back in her chair and surveyed the table. The bowl was empty and both the glass of juice and the bitter coffee had been drained. She rubbed her stomach happily and sighed. Then the door opened.

She turned so fast she almost fell right off the chair. Silver Glove stood in the doorway; her stomach did a backflip like it always did when he walked into the room. But it settled down quickly enough when she saw his three colleagues behind him. They entered her room and grabbed her; she was lifted almost completely off the floor as they started pulling her towards the door.

'What's going on?' She looked confused. 'Why are you dragging
me?'

'Come with us, piggy. There is more to be done today than eat.'

The words stung, but she cast her eye back to the table and realised the food provided was always more than enough for two people. She always ate every last bite. She looked at the man who had spoken the cruel words. He was holding her left arm and his strong fingers were leaving marks on her flesh. He had bright blue eyes that were mesmerising to her. They were a shade that looked so familiar, yet she'd never seen eyes like them – they almost glowed.

She was still staring as they pulled her out of the room. She wanted to call out to the man who protected her, helped her, and made her feel like it was all okay. He was kinder than these men and she wanted to always be alone with him. Why did he bring them?

She opened her mouth, then realised she didn't even know his name. Caught off guard, her mouth hung open as she allowed herself to be dragged.

They hadn't been moving for very long before they reached a metal door. It looked unfriendly which she found particularly strange. How could a door be unfriendly? Such a ridiculous concept, yet here she was, faced with the meanest most unfriendly door she had ever seen.

The man with the tattoo opened it and they led her inside. She was walking under her own volition now, apparently trusted not to run away. The room was clinical, looked a lot like the infirmary in the complex. There were cabinets full of supplies and light boxes for looking at X-rays. Metal tables stood around the edges with rolls of blue paper and little instruments on top. Strangely, the one thing that stood out amongst all this equipment was the metal bed that stood in the centre of the room; terrifyingly, rows of metal spikes were arranged on mechanical arms above the bed.

The door closed behind her and she was pushed towards the bed.

'Lie down.' It was blue eyes. She slowly dragged her feet towards the bed but she was beginning to freeze. The horror of her situation was dawning on her and she felt utterly helpless and afraid. The realisation that whatever those spikes did they were going to do to her, was a harsh one indeed.

As her body started to shake, Silver Glove appeared beside her, gently taking her arm, helping her not to collapse with panic. He whispered in her ear, 'This is going to hurt Alissa and I'm sorry for that. I'm sorry they are here as well but they wanted to see your progress. There is nothing more I can do to protect you because you need to do this.'

She nodded as bravely as she could but was betrayed by the sob that escaped her lips. She lay down onto the cold metal bed and closed her eyes. She didn't have to look, they could do whatever they wanted to her, but she wouldn't watch and they couldn't force her to. This was her tiny victory, the minuscule bit of control she had over them. That thought alone was enough to help calm her.

The four men moved away and faced a control panel. Only Silver Glove turned to look at her as the man with the scar stabbed at buttons below the panel. The mechanical arms came to life and manoeuvred themselves so the spikes were strategically aimed at all her major muscle groups. Slowly they moved towards her, inch by inch, until she felt the cold tip of each spike gently touch her skin. They stopped moving and she sighed with relief. She couldn't bear to think that she was going to be impaled by this machine, and her eyes remained closed.

Suddenly each spike shot forward, only by a centimetre, but it was enough to penetrate though the skin and into her flesh. She screamed in pain and shock and her eyes flew open. And as electricity surged through her she thought about her control. That little bit of power. It had been stolen from her, she had nothing left.
Every few seconds, the machine sent a wave of current through each conductor, and as it pulsed deep into her muscles, stimulating them, encouraging them to grow and strengthen, she lost consciousness and everything went black.

She felt the comfort of her bed before she even realised she was awake. The last thing she remembered was the cold metal and the searing pain. She flinched at the memory.

When she opened her eyes she was back in her little room. The man with the silver glove sat beside her, holding her limp hand. Her eyes searched his face but he seemed unable to look at her. Instead, he stared at the hand he was holding.

'I'm sorry.' He truly looked it too. 'It was never going to be pleasant. I'm even sorrier that we will do it to you again before your time here comes to an end.'

Her tears started falling as he spoke.

'No, not again ...' she moaned.

'I will make this as easy as I can but I need you to understand that no matter what, I have to do my duty.'

She half-closed her eyes. It took all of her strength not to scream. Now it was her turn to look away. Leave, she silently prayed. Let me be alone. But she knew she didn't really want that. Throughout all of this, the man with the silver glove had helped her. He wasn't like the rest. She had a mission and so did he, but what about when it was all over? Would they be free to spend real time together? Would he be on the Ark? She couldn't bear to leave him behind now. This man was in her life, and although she didn't even know his name, she could see the good in him. It hurt him to do these things to her, and they were going to carry on. With that thought fresh in her mind, tears fell from her eyes and she wept silently.

In the days that followed, her torment continued; they stopped only for food and sleep. She lost count of the number of times they had tortured her for 'the greater good'. She ached all over and the repeated pain all but scrambled what little she had left of her internal clock. She felt like it had been months, years even, since she'd been outside. But she knew it wasn't possible, the

Ark was due to leave just under two weeks from when she was drafted.

She didn't think of it as kidnap anymore. She had been chosen for a mission. This wasn't a prison; it was her own personal training facility.

Towards the end she became stronger. She lay silently, defiantly, as electricity coursed through her muscles. She couldn't see him but Silver Glove watched over her proudly.

During their short breaks from the screen she would be eager to get back in, to learn more. The food had been having an effect as well. Her body was leaner, the extra weight she had been carrying was gone and she was stronger now. On the final day, the arms above the bed were retracted for the last time. Silver Glove walked over to Alissa and pulled her to her feet. There were a million words in her mind that she wanted to say, all fighting to be the first out. He looked deep into her eyes for the first time in what felt like an eternity.

'Thank you,' she heard herself say.

LAUNCH MINUS FIVE

CHAPTER ELEVEN

GARRET SAT IN HIS LIVING SPACE WITH A LARGE glass of Class One whiskey.

This was the strong stuff. It was given to him when he reached twenty-one by his father. He had never opened it though – he wasn't a big drinker usually, but he needed something to numb his mind.

On the coffee table in front of him was a disk; just a disk, nothing scary or unusual about it. He had found it behind his door one evening when he arrived home.

There was nothing particularly remarkable about the day he found it. He had been at his office. His search for evidence had ended fruitlessly and he had pretty much given up on the idea. Andover was his captain and he would have to trust him. So he had carried on with his regular duties, handing out the promotions, working on the shifts, overseeing the crew's duty roster and the ship's passenger manifest.

He'd even gone to the canteen with some of the senior crew to socialise, which was very unlike him. But he thought: These are going to be the only people I'll ever see for the rest of my life so I'd better make sure I like them! Then the rest of them had continued on one of the complex bars and Garret had said his goodbyes.

He had walked home in silence along the busy corridors; he was smiling at strangers, tapping his fingers in his pocket to a tune that was stuck in his head, and just generally being a happy man. Then he arrived home. The door slid open and as he walked through he nearly stood on the damn thing. Nearly crushed it into shards with his boots. If only he had, he wouldn't be in this position now.

The thing caught his eye and he grabbed it and walked to his terminal. After placing it in the reader he went and sat on the couch, watching the blank screen intently. After a few moments of nothing, and just when he was about to give up, a grainy image appeared in front of him, a satellite picture taken on the day of the first Ark launch.

He watched as the picture came to life. He saw the Ark appear as a little blip of light and enter Earth's orbit. There is stayed for a few minutes – probably, he thought, getting final instructions from Ground Control. Then, as the blip moved away from the planet, it turned momentarily into a much bigger blip of light, and vanished.

He sat, open-mouthed, as the image changed to two years later, the next launch. He watched as again the blip flashed and disappeared.

The Arks were being destroyed. Surely the captain must know about this. Why didn't he tell me?

That's when he was shown the truth, page after page of documents scrolling down the monitor, showing that each captain had sabotaged their own ship. They were part of an underground movement that believed the human race should live and die in their own world. They were afraid the Lord wouldn't follow them to a new planet. So they were 'saving' all those migrants who would have lived without God – an outdated concept nowadays. Religion had faded after the Incident and the few who still believed while the bombs fell, turned their backs when they saw the number of the dead. They didn't want to believe in a God that would allow this to happen.

He drank deeply from the glass and stared at his terminal. He had watched the destruction of the Arks again and again, pored over the documents. They said the captain had killed his wife to spare her from the future.

Garret had been here for days now, in a drunken stupor, barely eating, surviving on cheap drinks. Only when he had run out of everything else did he open the Class One. He needed an ally.

Someone he could go to with this, and figure out a plan. Usually he would go straight to his captain. Not now. He considered going to another senior member of the crew but couldn't think who would be able to help him.

I'll look through the manifest later. Now I need sleep.
His eyes closed and the drink fell from his hand.

***

I need to see Shem. Alissa could think of nothing else as her feet took her along the corridors of the complex. They had released her at five in the morning and told her she had to do her duty. It was a phrase that had been drilled into every man, woman and child in the complex.

Always do your duty to the complex. Always protect the complex. Lately, however, the mantra had begun to seem less relevant. After all, people kept leaving the planet, and what good was the complex to them then?

The question was, could she do her duty now? Back in the familiar halls it became impossible to recall those feelings of determination and certainty. She wanted to see his face, and then she'd know.

After everything she had been through this week, she needed him more than ever. She wandered the corridor towards his quarters. *If I see him and tell him everything and he still wants to be around me, then it's all okay.* She was terrified that he would judge her. And if he judged her too harshly surely Ham would too. Ham's respect for life ran deeper than anyone else she knew. *If Shem tells me to stop...I will.*

A conflict raged within her.

'They said they would kill you if you didn't help.'

Maybe they were just trying to scare me?

'They've wasted so much time on you. They'll be mad if you run.'

I don't want to be a murderer.

A murderer. Not an assassin, but the cold hard killer they had turned her into. Is that what Silver Glove had done to her? The man who seemed to care about her, who held her hand while she slept. If he was right about everything then she had to kill the captain, to save Shem and Ham.

Alissa looked more determined than ever. *I will tell him everything, and if he judges me, too bad. I'm doing this to save him.*

***

Shem was feeling a little the worse for wear. The bosses always gave time off to those who wanted it, if they made it onto the Ark; to allow them, they said, to enjoy their last few weeks of Earth.

He hadn't left his quarters in a week, but it had been a glorious week and a long time coming in his opinion. He opened his eyes and squinted around the mess that used to be his room. Clothes were everywhere and things had been knocked over and broken. 'It looks like I've been robbed!' he said aloud, and chuckled.

He was surprised at the mess; he didn't think he'd been that drunk. He rolled over in bed and saw Sophia, still sleeping, wrapped up in his sheets. He smiled and decided that the proper thing to do in this situation was go make the lady some coffee.

He walked to his little kitchenette and pushed a toggle switch on the wall. A Coffee Friend had been installed in every home in New Amerland; the government felt that everyone, no matter how poor, should have access to free coffee. It helped to start the day off right.

Shem hummed the Coffee Friend jingle and sat himself down at his little metal table and rested his head in his hands. As the machine bubbled, he thought about the night he had met Sophia. She was really very pretty and it had been a long time since he'd been with a woman. That's when he was smacked with the realisation that Alissa was the only girl he really knew. This disturbed him a little because he'd always been popular with the ladies in his teens. After all, he thought with his customary modesty, he was tall, good-looking and very friendly but then he met Alissa, and he focused so hard on being there for her that all his old friends moved on with their lives and left him behind. That's how a computer technician ended up best friends with the mechanics.

His outlook changed. All his old friends were stuck up and pretentious. Shem wasn't like that, he was kind and funny and people enjoyed being around him. Alissa and Ham were the only other people who shared those qualities.

The coffee machine buzzed to let Shem know the coffee was ready and it snapped him out of his daydream. He poured a couple of cups and headed back to the bedroom. Walking through the door he saw Sophia slowly waking up and getting her bearings. Her eyes were drawn to the movement at the doorway and there she saw Shem, naked and holding two cups of steaming coffee. She smiled and beckoned him to the bed.

He walked over and handed her a warm cup. No words were exchanged between them and a slight awkwardness had begun to develop. Shem was about to ask her if she was going to spend another day with him when he was interrupted by the doorbell.

He jumped up, pulled on a pair of pyjama pants and jogged down the hallway to the door. He pressed the panel and the door slid open to reveal a young and quite beautiful woman.

'Hey Shem.' She smiled.

'Alissa?' She looked so different. Her hair was hanging down past her shoulders and looked clean for once. She was thinner too; how on earth had she done that in a week? Then there was her face. She looked older but somehow the same. He was confused by her and it made him uncomfortable.

'What are you doing here?' Shem's surprise caught her off-guard; it wasn't the welcome home she had expected.

'I ... um ... I needed to talk to you. I've had a very strange week
and ...'

Alissa stopped talking. She had glanced over Shem's shoulder and seen a woman, naked but for a sheet around her shoulders, walking past the bedroom door.

'Oh, I didn't know you had someone round.' She smiled. 'She's pretty, well done!' She winked at him and turned away and started walking down the hallway towards her quarters.

Shem stood in the open doorway and watched her. She didn't look back. She never does, he thought.

'That was Alissa, wasn't it?' Sophia was standing behind him.

'How do you know?'

'She's kinda pretty, in a plain way, I guess,' she said harshly. Shem was staring at her with a questioning look.

'You were saying her name in your sleep. All night. Look, Shem, I wasn't looking for anything long term here. I was enjoying myself but I'm not going to be someone that you can pretend is her. If you really want her, go and get her.'

With that Sophia turned away and headed back to Shem's room, presumably to find her clothes. Shem decided to give her some privacy and to let her keep her dignity. He hid in the kitchen until she left.

***

Alissa held back her tears. She wasn't upset about the woman,
Shem was a grown-up and he could do what he liked. She was upset because she needed her best friend and he wasn't there for her. You're so selfish, she told herself. But she needed someone to help her; she needed to tell someone what she knew. She was beginning to doubt her abilities and wonder whether she could ever do this

alone. But who could she turn to now? And who would believe her? She leant against a wall and just as the first tear started to fall she heard a voice.

'Don't cry. You're too beautiful to cry.'

She smiled and turned to face him. He walked over to her and wiped a tear with his gloved hand. 'Don't cry.'

'You've never called me beautiful.'

He smiled at her with that unusual smile. 'You never needed me to.' She looked into his eyes. They were such deeps pools on his face, and she really thought she might drown in them. When it became too much, her gaze dropped to his feet.

'I don't understand this. We were down in your training rooms for what felt like months, how has it only been a week? How can I be ready in a week?'

Alissa's questions were fair enough. How was it possible to train an assassin in seven days? But then, it hadn't been days in the facility – she'd been there much longer than that. Silver Glove sighed deeply and the protective look on his face was replaced with concern. He didn't want to reveal this information.

'Alissa, we have a device that enables time to run differently. What feels like weeks in the facility is only a matter of days here in your complex.'

It was Alissa's turn to look concerned. 'How can that be? Technology like that doesn't even exist and the Research and Development City shut down after the Incident. The only thing to be designed since then is the Ark.'

'We are a well-hidden and well-funded organisation, Alissa. Your government has never been entirely honest with you and as a result of that, my team is able to put plans like this into place.' He took a step closer to her.

'You have become someone new Alissa, you must embrace your new strength. You're a very special young woman.'

'I'm not special,' she said defiantly. 'I'm just desperate.'

Silver Glove lifted her chin so she was looking him in the eyes.

'You are special. And beautiful, and strong.'

The reassurance was everything she craved from Shem, and she succumbed to his complements once again. This was his power over her.

'If you can take care of this then I'll take care of you forever. Do you understand that?'

Alissa nodded. 'But I don't know that I can do it alone.'

Silver Glove pulled a personal terminal from his pocket and showed it to Alissa.

'This man will help you. Go to him.'

Moments later she was alone in the hallway, but now she knew where to find help and with a new sense of determination, she headed back to her apartment.

CHAPTER TWELVE

SHEM SAT ON HIS BED, THINKING ABOUT THE NIGHT before. He knew he was lucky he hadn't called out Alissa's name in the throes of passion – after all, he hadn't been thinking about Sophia. How had this happened? And where had Alissa been? He was worried for her but at the same time, too embarrassed to call her. Plus, she'd know Sophia had left and she might suspect Shem's feelings, and that was too much to think about right now.

He walked over to his screen and called Ham. He needed to see a friendly face and Ham's was his favourite. After a few minutes the screen clicked and Ham's round happy face appeared before him.

'Shem! You won't believe where I am!' Shem played along.

'I don't know … the garage?'

'Nope! Try again.' Ham's smile grew wider and Shem's followed suit. He loved Ham's enthusiasm for life.

'Saime's Bar?'

'Haha, wrong again!'

Shem started to laugh. 'Okay, I give up Ham. Where are you?'

'Look out your window!'

Shem looked over to the window then back at the screen. Ham was nodding furiously so Shem walked over and looked out over the dusty streets. His room was on the edge of the complex so he really got one of the best views of the old city.

As his eyes scanned the view he noticed something glinting in one of the old towers. It was a light flashing, maybe a torch of some kind. Someone was clearly in there.

'Ham? Is that you over there?'

'Yeah!' Ham almost screamed in delight.

'How the Hell did you get in there?'

'I'll show you. Meet me in the canteen in ten minutes.'

'How are you going to get to the canteen that quickly?'

Just trust me will you!' With that there was a click and Shem stood staring at a blank screen.

**

Garret was walking down a grey corridor that led to the subway alley. A shudder ran through him as he realised he would have to use the subway, yet again. He was slightly more sober now and had made the decision that showing Andover the footage would be a good idea.

This could all be an innocent mistake and the captain could potentially have a perfectly good explanation for all this, or he could simply be oblivious, like Garret.

While his thoughts were elsewhere a girl stepped in front of him. He stopped suddenly and made an attempt to walk past her. She blocked his path. Garret looked her over and thought, she's young, twenty-five tops. With long brown hair that fell in waves over her shoulders and almost down to her waist, and blue eyes that glinted in the artificial light, she did look slightly younger but Garret was good with ages. She was wearing all black – a tank top and tight combat pants tucked into large army-issue boots. She looked like trouble.

As he was looking her over he realised she was armed and in an attempt to avoid any kind of altercation, he simply said, 'Excuse me Miss, I am in a rush.' Again he attempted to sidestep her and again she blocked his way. She knows, he thought. She knows about the footage.

'You are Garret, First Officer of the new Ark. Is that correct?'

For a moment he considered lying to her but he knew that would probably end badly for him so he simply sighed and said, 'Yes, that is me. And who might you be?'

He made the conscious decision to stand his ground as it seemed like the appropriate course of action. The girl stared at him for a second before she replied.

'My name is Alissa. I'm going to be a passenger on your ship.'

A new thought entered his mind. She didn't make the grade. She's going to threaten her way on.

'I'm glad to hear it, miss. Now if you don't mind, I must be going. I have important business to attend to. That is, if you want the ship to leave on time.' He chuckled nonchalantly and looked at her, hoping that she would take her cue and leave him alone. If she was anything other than completely serious she'd take this opportunity and go.

'No. You can't go. You have to help me, Garret. Something has happened and I need your help.'

'I don't understand.' He was less worried now. Perhaps she didn't know about the Arks. Did she actually want to help him? She looked up and down the corridor and lowered her voice as if the place were filled with spies, although Garret saw no one.

'We cannot talk freely here. Please follow me to my quarters.'

Garret took a deep breath. This is it, he thought. I'm either going to save the day, or I'm heading to my own execution. He followed her, but only because he didn't think he had much choice.

Alissa paced her living area, gun in hand, while Garret sat silently on her couch. She was trying to put her thoughts in some kind of order.

She had the training, the strength and the ability to complete this mission, but she lacked conviction. She knew that – it was obvious – but Garret was the last piece of her personal puzzle and in his possession was the evidence, the one thing she had yet to see. The only problem was, she wasn't sure she wanted to see it. It would change everything, make this entire endeavour real and be the true start of her mission.

Eventually she turned and faced him. He was essentially just a tired old man; could he handle this burden? He smelled of alcohol and looked a mess. He definitely needed a shower and some sobering up. But now wasn't the time.

He looked in her eyes and didn't like what he saw. It was as if there wasn't a person there, just anger and violence walking around in human form. Who did this to you, child? The silence was uncomfortable and he willed her to talk so that he would know she was real.

Finally, she must have finished wrestling with her conscience because she raised the gun and pointed it at his face.

'Tell me what you know, Garret.'

'About what?' He didn't want to throw the information he had at her; he didn't even know if that was the reason for his 'arrest'.

'Don't mess me around, old man. Tell me what you know.' Every word was punctuated by a little tilt of the gun. He looked down the barrel and back at her. One wrong move and she would kill him – she looked entirely capable of it.

You have to tell me what you need,' he said. 'And trust me when I say, if I can help you, I will.' He was sincere but he could see her studying his face for any sign of defiance.

She must have been satisfied because she replaced the gun in its holster at her waist and sat beside him.

'It's about the captain.' She turned her head and looked at him. 'I need to know what you know about him.'

Garret shifted uncomfortably. Was he going to tell this maniac what he knew?

'I know a great deal about the captain but I'm more interested in you.'

He was feeling brave now that the gun was no longer aimed at his face, and the great diplomatic skills that his father instilled in him came to the surface.

'Tell me, Alissa. Why is a young, intelligent and, dare I say, beautiful girl like yourself carrying a gun and threatening the first officer of the very ship you want to escape on?'

Alissa looked at the floor in front of her; the compliment fell on deaf ears, which was a testament to how committed she was to the cause. 'I need to know about the captain. I have a mission.' She spoke quietly, deliberately. There was still a part of her that respected authority. 'I have job to do, and I know you can help me. I was told.'

'Told by whom?'

Alissa's stomach flipped as Silver Glove came into her mind, but he was her secret. 'I can't tell you that.' She looked at his lined face, at the tired and rheumy eyes. 'What I can tell you is that your captain wants us all dead. He wants the Ark to fail. This is the human race that's at stake. It's our last chance of survival and I'm not going to let Clarke Andover destroy it. Garret, we have to try to stop him. So please, tell me what you know.'

Garret let out a deep sigh. It was time, he supposed. The disk was in his jacket pocket. He reached in and pulled it out, holding it at Alissa's eye line so she could get a good look at it. Her gaze followed him as he walked to her wall screen and popped the disk into the drive. He pressed a few buttons and the footage of all the Ark incidents played in sequence. As Alissa watched the screen, Garret watched her – he wanted to see her reaction, he still wasn't sure he was doing the right thing.

When the first ship was destroyed she gasped, then as horror turned to realisation she tried to come to terms with the implications. This was going to be difficult for her. This was going to mean accepting her lot in life and becoming an assassin. She rose to her feet and walked a few steps towards the screen. As the last Ark exploded her face crumpled and she fell to her knees. All those people, dead. Ham's family were on those ships, and now they're gone. She was going to have to tell him. Oh God.

Garret ran to her and dropped down on one knee. He put his arms around her and held her while she cried. Between sobs she murmured, 'I didn't want it to be true ... I wanted you to tell me I was wrong ... I don't want to have to ...' The end of her sentence was lost in sobs.

She suddenly felt small and vulnerable, like a child. Garret sat silently and stroked her hair while she cried.

***

Shem walked into the canteen and his eyes scanned the room for his portly friend; he couldn't see him so he assumed he was there first. He smiled. I knew he couldn't get here in ten minutes.

He walked over to the food line and joined the end of the queue. He hadn't eaten yet today and his stomach was being unusually boisterous in trying to remind him. He was nearing the front when Ham suddenly appeared by his side, making him jump.

'Hey, Shem.'

'Jeez Ham, you scared me!' Shem looked at Ham with concern: he was, to say the least, looking dishevelled. 'Are you okay buddy?'

'Oh, yeah, I'm good. Hungry though.'

They reached the front of the queue and ordered their breakfast. They walked silently down the line and Shem paid for their food. They sat down at an empty table.

'So, how did you get over there?' asked Shem through a mouthful of oats.

'Tunnels.'

'What tunnels? Like the ones the UOs hide in?' Shem was beginning to look worried and his voice had become a loud whisper.

No, they're like an underground maze of corridors and rooms. They cover the entire city, even beyond. Secret tunnels, Shem. They're empty.'

'That doesn't mean they're secret.' Shem's voice was thick with concern. 'Have you been on the enhancers again?'

Ham looked offended. 'Don't you get it? We only have a week left on Earth. Why don't we use it to explore the old city? It will be the three of us, you, me and Alissa.'

Shem frowned at Alissa's name. 'I don't know if she would be interested.'

'Why not?'

'I saw her this morning. She looked different. I ... I think she's busy.' Shem started trying to think up reasons not to invite her. His vain assumption was that she was hurt by his behaviour with Sophia.

He hadn't figured out how to fix their relationship yet, and now she seemed so different, he had no idea where to start. He looked across the table at Ham. She was his friend too and he had a right to know what was going on with her. But Shem didn't want to share all of this with him; not yet anyway.

'Okay then, just us?' Ham still looked hopeful.

'Sure Ham, just us.' Shem smiled and took another mouthful of

oats.

After breakfast, the two friends walked in silence towards the nearest airlock. Shem was thinking about Alissa and Ham was scared that if he started talking he'd reveal all the secrets he'd found. So neither said a word.

When they arrived at the doorway Ham touched the panel. It slid back to reveal a little room with spacesuits hung on pegs around all four walls. They took one each and pulled them over their clothes and checked each other for breaches. It was a safety measure you were supposed to adhere to every time you left the complex.

Ham was usually alone but he always checked himself as best he could.

When Ham pressed the buttons in a four-digit sequence, one door shut and a few seconds later the other opened with a whoosh, sucking in dust from the grey and deserted cityscape beyond so that it swirled around the two men. They stood motionless, waiting for the dust to clear and their vision to adjust.

They walked out into the dry landscape and Shem faltered. He'd never actually been outside before and it took him a few moments to come to terms with it. Ham waited in tactful silence as Shem gasped at the view. It was so different out here, no walls or ceilings surrounding you, just wide open space and huge, beautiful buildings designed by architects with a wonderful vision of what the future might have held. Sadness seemed to hang over the place like a shroud.

Shem gathered his composure and took a few steps to stand beside his companion. They glanced at each other and started walking. Ham was half a step in front, leading the way to the panel. Shem paid no attention to the direction they were walking. Instead, he took in his surroundings. His eyes traced the buildings on either side, from street level up to a narrow opening far above and what might once have been blue sky. 'Skyscrapers,' he mumbled to himself. Everything was covered in a thick layer of dust that hadn't been disturbed in decades.

They made their way through the city and reached the panel. Shem saw it a few minutes before they arrived – a patch of ground with all the dirt and dust scraped away leaving the panel exposed. Ham stepped up and pressed the buttons he had programmed. The hatch slid open and Ham lowered himself down onto the ladder below. Shem followed him down.

They wandered the corridors together, laughing and joking. It felt like when they had first met, when they had no cares and life was an adventure. They were children again.

Ham chased his best friend down a long hallway, laughing so hard tears rolled down his face. Shem looked over his shoulder and smiled.

He was running fast and as he reached a door he quickly grabbed the handle, turned it and threw himself against the door. It flew off its hinges and Shem went flying into the room, landing on top of the door, laughing like a maniac. Ham leant against the opening, breathing heavily and still laughing. Then he looked around. As he took in his surroundings his face became more serious. Shem followed his gaze.

The walls were covered with pictures of Captain Andover. Him and his son, him alone, him working in his office, walking down a corridor – every detail of this man's life was being documented. Shem scrambled to his feet and turned in a small circle, taking in every detail of the room.

What is this?' Ham barely whispered.

'I don't know, Ham. Not sure I want to.'

Shem noticed a folder on a table at the far end of the room. He walked over and lifted it. He opened the folder and began to scan the contents. His eyes became wide and his face contorted, first with confusion, then panic, and finally anger. As Ham watched, his frown deepened.

'What does it say?'

'Ham, we have to go now.'

Seventy floors high, the most beautiful skyscraper in the centre of
the old city cast its long shadow on the landscape below. Though streaked and blackened with dust from the fallout, it still looked to be in good condition. It was dead straight all the way from street level to the sixty-eighth floor, but the top two levels were special. They had been

designed almost one hundred years ago by the late Rupert Maddox, an architect with a vision of the future unlike anyone else.

The giant glass dome ceiling sat upon two floors of open space and had housed a unique botanical garden. He knew that one day people wouldn't be able to venture outside, so he brought nature in. His designs inspired the huge gardens housed within each Ark. The designers said it helped with morale and it was a genius way to provide oxygen and remove carbon dioxide in a contained vessel. Inside the tower, one thing was immediately noticeable – it was completely airtight and every surface was clean. None of the poisonous particles had penetrated to the inside so it was possible to walk around without a protective suit.

It wasn't possible to access the tower from the city – not that anyone had tried. The secret tunnel system was the only way in, which was easy enough when you knew the way.

From a west-facing, floor to ceiling window on the fifty-second floor of the Maddox building, there was clear view of a beautiful apartment building known as Swan Towers, and if your scope was good enough, as Alissa's was, you could see right into Captain Andover's home.

For hours she watched him as he read his books, cooked, danced with his son to music she was too far away to hear. She would wait until she was quite sure he was alone. She would not do this in front of his son. Traumatising a little boy was not high on her list of things to do. Last resort, she told herself. Last resort.

She followed him with the crosshairs from room to room. Every time she moved the rifle made automatic adjustments in her arms. She was lying on the floor with her eye pressed against the scope, watching him, her index finger barely touching the trigger. She was ready to shoot when the moment was right. But still she waited.

The man and his boy had made their way into the living space and were now sitting in overstuffed chairs, facing each other and reading books. It unsettled Alissa deeply to see the boy so clearly enjoying the company of his father.

She thought about her own father. He had died when she was only thirteen. It was too young to be alone. Her mother died during childbirth and while she sometimes felt sad about it, she never felt cheated. Her father had created the perfect family life for her. For hours they would sit and talk about his work. He had owned a small engineering works, and had taught Alissa everything she knew about ships and engines, hoping that one day she would follow in his footsteps and take over the business. He was regarded as the best independent mechanic around, and people would travel all the way from the other side of the city, sometimes even further, to have him look at their little ships.

But when he died, Alissa was still too young to take on a business, and eventually the Complex Board of Governors stepped in and issued a closure notice. She had kept the sign from the front entrance and put it in her room. Just a small, painted wooden sign with 'CAPT. ENOCH'S ENGINES' painted in beautiful script. Her mother had done that, many years before she was born.

He called himself a captain, told her stories of when he was a young man, tales of adventure and excitement, danger and love, of being a captain was how he'd met her mother, how they'd settled down and eventually had Alissa.

She didn't know exactly how much of it was true – her father did like to exaggerate and there was always the chance that he was just an engineer on board a ship. She could've looked it up, walked down to the library and searched for her father, but she didn't really want to know the truth. Captain Enoch's tales were too wonderful to give up.

Alissa had become a mechanic, just as she had promised.
Sometimes she visited his old shop. It had been turned into little box rooms for visitors to the complex quite a few years ago, but she still liked to sit out front in the large metallic hall on the cold little bench and pretend she was little again. It had been too long since she'd done that.

The captain rose to his feet and she snapped out of her daydream. Eagle-eyed, she watched as he walked to the kitchenette and made coffee. It looked like he was preparing for a long night. Not long now, she thought.

***

Garret was sitting in his living space. He had left Alissa's a few hours earlier. She said she needed some time to herself and who was he to argue? He was thinking of all the things that had happened so far. It's not too late to stop this. He wasn't a killer, or an accessory.

Am I having second thoughts? He didn't know. He could still back out, go back to Alissa and help her. Or he could talk to her and they could go and see the captain, talk to him and find out what was really going on.

His screen buzzed to life and his eyes flew to it; the sound signalled the emergency channel. Frowning, he walked over, pressed Receive on the panel and raised an eyebrow as Shem's face appeared before him. 'Chief Navigation Officer Shem here, Sir, with an urgent message.' The boy saluted.

'Go ahead, Chief.'

'Sir, I have reason to believe that the captain's life is in danger. I have found evidence of an assassination plot. Protocol states that in the event of a threat against the captain, all available crew will immediately be called in, ready to provide protection.'

Such a young man, thought Garret, filled with ambition, always going by the book. He'd probably make an excellent captain one day.

'I am aware of protocol, Chief. I will take care of this and I trust you will have enough discretion to keep this to yourself.'

'Yes, Sir.'

'Good. Garret out.' And with that Garret pressed the same button and the screen went blank. He leant against the wall and took a deep breath. 'This is it. Now. This is it.'

CHAPTER THIRTEEN

'HOW'S THE BOOK KID?' THE QUESTION CAUGHT Louis off guard; he had immersed himself in a world of monsters and heroes and had almost completely forgotten his father was there.

'It's good. There are things called Elves and they hate these Dwarves, but they have to work together to stop this huge monster.'

Louis's face was so animated when he talked about books.

Clarke smiled. 'Which do you prefer?'

'Dwarves are way better, because they're stronger and they have much cooler weapons.'

Clarke's eyes dropped back down to his own book. It's was a historical retelling of the Incident from a survivor's point of view. Not the most interesting of tales but enough to keep him occupied.

The little digital clock on the wall gave out a short buzz indicating that it was 11 p.m.

'Lou, it's getting pretty late and I think you know what that means.' Clarke went to close his book.

'Okay Dad.' Louis jumped to his feet and put his book onto the little table between them. 'Goodnight,' he said.

'Bye son. I'll look in shortly.'

Clarke felt a pang of loneliness. He often felt it when Louis wasn't around, and he always felt like he wasn't coming back. He was an obedient boy though, he didn't argue, never whinged, an angel really.

He wasn't always that way. Back when his mother was alive he would run riot, wanting attention from everyone all the time, a real handful.

Then he just changed. His doctors thought it was trauma from the accident and Clarke tended to agree. Louis had been through a lot.

He shook the thoughts from his mind and had just returned to his book when a loud ringing caught his attention. He walked to the front door and punched the lock sequence into the panel, and the door slid open to reveal a sweating and clearly panic-stricken Garret. He moved past Clarke and allowed the door to slide shut behind him.

'Captain, I have some disturbing news. Do you have a safe room?'

'Of course, follow me.'

Alissa watched as Garret was guided through the captain's home.

'What is he telling you, captain?' she whispered.

Clarke led the way down the small hallway, stopping at Louis' room. 'I'm sure you won't object to me bringing him? If I'm in danger then so is he.'

Garret nodded. 'Of course, Captain.'

Clarke slipped into the room. It had only been five minutes but Louis was already fast asleep.

'Come on son, time to wake up.'

Clarke's voice was barely audible but Louis' eyes flew open and he sat up. 'Is everything okay Dad?'

'Yeah, but he need to move into the safe room. Come on.'

He took his son's hand and led him back out into the hallway, and from there the three of them proceeded to the office at the end.

'Your office is your safe room?' Garret eyed the large windows and thought how safety was a relative concept. Not that this should bother him – it would make things a thousand times easier if someone shot the captain dead while he was here as a witness.

'No Garret, it's not.'

Clarke walked over to his bookcase and pressed a button underneath the middle shelf. It slid open to reveal a large doorway.

Now Garret was impressed.

'This' – he motioned the others through – 'is my safe room'.

Garret looked inside. It was small and the walls, floor and ceiling were solid concrete. He stepped in and looked at what appeared to be the basics: a couple of chairs, table and food supplies. But it also had a large computer panel beneath multiple terminals.

'Okay, Captain. You must remain in here until I return with a security team.'

'I understand, Garret. Find out who is responsible for this threat, my friend. Please.'

Garret nodded, turned and stepped through the door. It closed heavily behind him. The bookcase slid back into place hiding the safe room once again. The first officer walked through the captain's home to his living space. He pressed a few buttons on the panel and the screen lit up. Then he waited as the terminal buzzed. Alissa's face flashed up.

'What the hell are you doing?' Anger was etched into her face. She had answered the call on a personal terminal and Garret could see from the backdrop that she was in an old office building.

'I might ask you the same thing.'

She sighed and lifted the rifle into view. Garret's eyes widened.

'You … you're going to shoot him?'

'I was, until you showed up. Where did he go? There's only one
way in and out of that place.'

'He's in his safe room. Surrounded by concrete and steel. An impenetrable fortress, I would say.'

Alissa's jaw dropped. 'You warned him? You bastard.'

It was Garret's turn to be angry. 'I had no choice. My navigation chief discovered the plot and told me everything. Protocol dictates that all crew members must immediately report for duty and that I must inform the captain. Can you imagine how this would've turned out if I had just kept it to myself?'

He was right. She knew he was, but it didn't mean she liked it.

'This just became a thousand times more impossible. You know
that, don't you?'

'Yes.' The answer was more of a sigh than a word. 'I do, however, have an alternative plan. Can you meet me in the library in one hour?'

Alissa nodded, then hit the Off button on the communicator and the screen went black.

She took a deep breath and rose to her feet. Silver Glove had given her all she would need to accomplish her mission. Tucked safely into a sheath attached to her calf was a short, serrated knife. Her thighs were adorned with holsters in which nestled two guns, one on each side. Her pants had gone from baggy cargo pants to tight lycra which gave her a better range of movement.

She inspected her reflection in the window and realised that she didn't look like herself anymore. She was armed to the teeth, with her long hair flowing freely down her back. She looked like the killer she had become. She closed her eyes but the image of herself had burned its way into her psyche. What would Ham say if her saw her now?

Would he even recognise her?

The route to the library was a short one. She would run down to the tunnels, cross the underground network and come out round the corner. As she set off, her eyes were focused on the direction she was heading and her ears were ready to pick up anything that sounded threatening. She took long deliberate steps, turned a corner and saw the doorway to the library. In front of it were a dozen armed men and in the centre, looking directly at her, was Garret.

Had he lost his nerve and called security to take her away? She considered running. She was much faster now and she could probably hide for a while, but the computer would always find her. Meanwhile,

Garret had spotted her and he called her name. She sighed and walked over.

'Alissa, this is the security team that I have assigned to you. Now follow me inside for a briefing.'

They all followed Garret as he led them through the library into a back room. It was dimly lit with a huge table in the middle. It was designed for people to meet and discuss books and great writers, not to discuss a murder plot.

Most of them sat at the table and looked around. Garret chose to remain standing. He paced the room as he spoke. 'I would like to start by saying that due to her diligence, training and devotion to duty, Ms Alissa Namaah has been promoted to Chief of Security. I trust any problems you have will be dealt with efficiently.' He took a moment to look at the surprise etched across her face.

'I have assembled you to complete an important mission. To protect the captain.' Alissa's face went from surprise to confusion. As she stared, open-mouthed, at Garret, he continued.

'This morning I received a disturbing message, a message of which, by now, you should all be aware.' There were murmurs from the men and women round the table. Obviously when the security alert went out the security team was notified. Of course, thought Alissa. They had to go through the motions – it would be too suspicious if they didn't.

'There is evidence of a plot to murder Captain Andover,' continued Garret, 'and we cannot allow this to happen. The Chief Navigation Officer found this.' He pushed a file he had been holding into the middle of the table. All eyes were on the file except Alissa's. Hers were locked on Garret.

'We will be heading to the captain's home to retrieve him from his safe room. We will be escorting him to an underground bunker, where he will remain until launch day – and we shall be with him. I'm afraid there is no time to say your goodbyes to loved ones. Your loyalty to your captain starts now.'

There were murmurs from some of the team. A few had no family, so the idea of beginning their mission immediately didn't really affect them. Some of them, on the other hand, were devoted to their families and had plans for their last week together. They were the heartbroken ones.

Garret reached across the table and picked up the file. 'Gentlemen, your only job is to protect the captain. We leave shortly. Dismissed.'

Alissa and Garret followed the team in silence for a few minutes. He knew she wanted to say something so he waited until she spoke.

'Garret, why are you doing this?'

'Because protocol states that in the event of a threat to the captain, we must all do our duty.'

'I don't understand.'

'When you are in the bunker, there will be no escaping. The security team are strong but they are by no means, how shall I put it...clever. They will follow your orders and mine. Killing him will be quite simple.'

'I hope you're right.'

CHAPTER FOURTEEN

HAM AND SHEM WALKED ALONG THE CORRIDOR towards the canteen. It was getting light, neither of them had slept all night and they were both hungry. They walked in silence, the events of the day still running through their minds. They heard the sound of heavy footfalls coming towards them from around the corner. They slowed down as a large security team came into view. Pressing themselves against the wall, they tried to give them as much space as possible. The men were followed by the first officer and a woman. Then Shem did a double take as he realised that it wasn't just any woman. It was Alissa – a heavily armed Alissa.

'Hey! Alissa! What're you doing?' Ham had recognised her too but wasn't lost for words like Shem. She looked over to him. Her face showed no recognition. She turned her head back in the direction she was walking and continued, without looking back.

'What the hell was that about?' Shem's voice was back with a vengeance.

'I don't know Shem. But she looks different. She looks mean!'

'Come on, we're going back underground.'

'Aw no! I'm getting real hungry Shem.' Ham's enhancers had worn off and he hadn't taken more. With sleep around the corner he'd assumed that it would've been a waste.

'This has something to do with the captain. Someone has done something to Alissa and we have to find out what it is.' With that, Shem stalked off down the corridor, and Ham followed close behind.

Alissa's heart was breaking as she walked. That was her family. Those two men were her only true companions and she had treated them like strangers. Garret noticed a change in her step and glanced in her direction. Her face was set in sheer determination – determination not to cry.

'Those gentlemen. They are your friends, aren't they?' Alissa nodded.

'It hurt you to disregard them as you did.'

She nodded again. There was a slight tremble to her lip and she fought with herself fiercely.

'They will understand. When this is all over they will understand your reasons and they will welcome you back into their hearts.'

'What about your friends?' She wanted to hurt him. She was angry and Garret was going to take the brunt of it.

'The life of a first officer is a lonely one.' Garret's face turned stony and Alissa took that to mean their conversation was over.

They made the uneventful journey back to the captain's quarters via the subway system. Since they were on official business they were able to secure a train car that was empty. They boarded the vehicle and grabbed hold where they could. Garret thought back to his journey to the library earlier in the day. As usual, the car had been full of people crushing each other, without a care for their fellow passengers. Garret found it distasteful.

They reached the captain's quarters and Garret entered the code on the door panel. It slid open and half the group entered the house. The rest remained in the hallway, standing guard.

Garret turned to the few that had followed him in.

'Gentlemen, remain here. Alissa, come with me.'

Alissa nodded and followed Garret out of the room. They walked down the hallway and continued to the office. Once inside, the first officer pressed the button on the bookcase and the door opened. The captain and his son were sitting inside reading books. Clarke jumped to his feet when the door opened, at looked at Garret.

'Louis, there are guards all over,' said Garret. 'Go gather your favourite possessions and return here.' The boy looked at his father, who nodded, then left to follow Garret's instructions.

The captain looked calmer, but then he noticed Alissa. 'Who is she? I don't recognise her from the manifest.'

'Captain, Alissa is Chief of Security.' Garret sounded so sure of himself that even Alissa believed him.

'No, Roberts is Chief. You don't think I know the chief officers on my ship?' He took a step back. 'What's going on Garret?'

'Robert's refused to come.'

'But protocol—'

'He has chosen to remain here on Earth with his family. It's his wife, you see – she didn't make it onto the Ark.' His performance was stunning. 'Alissa here has been training for a transfer for months now. I felt the time was right to give her a chance.'

I could do it, she thought. The captain and Garret were arguing about her but not paying the slightest bit of attention to her. I could pull out my gun, pull the trigger and it would be over. Her hand moved imperceptibly closer to her waist. We would tell everyone we found him dead. The tips of her fingers traced along the barrel of the gun. This is it! Her fingers curled round the grip and then she heard a voice.

'Dad?'

All three of them turned to face the child. Alissa's hand dropped to her side. Her heart was pounding; it was the second time she'd readied herself and it was making her go a little mad. She looked to Garret.

His strong face steadied her. He returned her gaze, almost looked like he'd known her plan and had kept the captain busy on purpose – but she could never do it now and he knew it.

'Louis!' Andover walked over to his son and wrapped his arms protectively around him. He lifted him off the ground. 'Do you have everything you need, kiddo?'

'Yeah Dad, it's all in my backpack.'

'Good.' He turned to Garret. 'Let's go.'

Garret walked past Clarke and led the way out, where they joined the rest of the security team. The captain seemed to relax a little when he saw the group of uniformed men that were sworn to protect him.

Garret walked into the centre of the room and commanded the attention of everyone gathered.

'Gentlemen, and Alissa, we are here today to get the captain to the bunker situated one point five miles below the launch site of the Ark. We must be ready for any attack. Be prepared to kill anyone who might be a threat. The mission is what matters. Let's go.'

The team surrounded the captain, walking him out of his home and leaving Alissa and Garret to bring up the rear. 'You forgot the part about the fate of the world being in our hands,' said Alissa, as she walked past the older man.

They left the captain's quarters and began their journey to the bunker. The assassin was relaxed; she knew nothing would happen on this journey and she allowed her thoughts to wander. She kept to the rear of the group as she didn't want to engage any of the team in idle chit chat and she especially didn't want to speak to the captain. The awe she had felt for him was gone. She walked quietly for a few minutes, then realised that the captain's son was beginning to slow down and she was catching up to him. She took a deep breath as he fell into step next to her.

'My name's Louis.' He kept his eyes on his father as he spoke.

'Alissa.' She looked down at him. He was scrawny and small.

'Are you going to take care of my dad?'

'Yes.'

'Can I help?' She continued to look down at him. She saw the fear in his eyes. 'I'm clever! I can do things with computers. You have to let me help.'

Alissa pulled her eyes away from his terrified face and looked at the captain. 'Okay. You can help.'

Louis smiled and hurried his walk to catch up with his father, slipping his fingers into the captain's hand. Alissa could that he was being protective, walking half a step ahead and never taking his eyes off his father. He was clearly devoted.

In any other time or place, Alissa would have savoured the view. There was no love stronger than that of a father. It was beautiful. If she was going to kill the captain, she would have to kill his son too.

Perhaps it would be kinder that way. After all, how would the boy survive without his father? He would end up homeless, starving or – the most likely scenario – dead. She would have to kill him but it would be done quickly, no suffering. If she did it right he wouldn't even know. This would be her secret though. Garret couldn't know about this; he wasn't a cruel man and she doubted that he could handle the guilt of murdering an innocent child.

This was why she had been trained. So she could make the decisions no one else could.

***

Shem made his way through the underground hallways with Ham following behind. His face was determined but his worried eyes gave him away. Alissa had never behaved that way before. Something had changed her and it had something to do with her visit to his home.

Shem kicked himself for not trying to stop her from leaving. Could he have prevented this, whatever this might be? She was with Garret so it was somehow related to the file he had found. Was this his fault?

That's why they were here now. They had to find out what had happened to her so they could help her.

'Shem?' His friend remained silent. 'Shem, where are we going?' Shem didn't even look at him. Hurt, Ham stopped following him and when Shem realised he was walking alone he turned around angrily.

'What is it Ham? What is so important?'

Ham flinched at his best friends' anger. Shem had never yelled at him before and it frightened him. Shem must've realised he'd gone too far because he stepped towards his friend. There was only silence between them now. Ham stared at his feet. He should've stopped asking questions. He should've stopped pestering Shem. That's why people didn't like to be around him, because he didn't know when to stop.

Shem was right in front of him now. His arms wrapped
themselves around his best friend and pulled him close. Ham's eyes started to brim as Shem held him. Shem hushed him as he started to cry. He was scared. Alissa was gone and the tunnels were scary and Shem was angry. He allowed the tears to fall without shame.

Shem took a deep breath and pulled away from his friend. His hands were still resting on the boy's shoulders. 'Okay now Ham. We need to calm down.'

Ham tried to hold back his tears.

'Alissa is in trouble and it's got something to do with the rooms we found. We have to see if there is anything else we can find out.' 'She didn't look in trouble. She looked scary.'

'I know.'

'So what if it's her? What if it's her we have to stop?'

'We won't.'

'We might have to.'

'We can't.'

'Why not?'

'Because she's the love of my life! Remember?' Shem sounded desperate. 'I told you about this. I'm in love with her so we have to save her. Simple as that. We have to help her. She'd do the same for us.'

'I understand.'

'Do you?' Shem's eyes searched Ham's face. Did he understand Shem's feelings? He didn't even know if Ham could fall in love. But this wasn't the time for a debate.

They started walking again, down the long hallway, but this time they walked side by side. Shem's thoughts were on Alissa. He was worried because Ham had a point. Alissa did look different. She looked like she was hardened but he didn't want to focus on it. The chances of it being her were so slim.

134

They reached a hallway that was filled with doors. The two friends looked at one another and silently decided to open every single door.

***

Alissa looked at Garret. He was staring at the door in front of him. He had entered the code and now they were waiting for the door to open. Clarke held his son's hand and looked around. His eyes met Alissa's and he smiled a genuine smile. He saw her as his protector. He was expecting her to save him, and she would've given anything to see that smile a week ago.

She looked down at her feet, embarrassed and unprepared. It was so easy to hate him when he wasn't there. Silver Glove and his team had told her all of the things Clarke Andover had done. He was an evil man who had been preparing for this day for years. To ensure the destruction of mankind. Maybe losing his wife pushed him over the edge, Alissa didn't even want to think about what would've happened if his son had died as well. He'd probably be blowing the Earth up too, just to make sure.

But it was hard to hate him when he looked at her with his brown eyes, so inviting and open, and his smile that was so genuine. He oozed charisma.

The door slid open, snapping Alissa's gaze away from the
captain's, and Garret stepped into the small room that would slowly descend two thousand metres to the underground bunker. He turned and motioned for the captain and Alissa to join him. Louis entered with his father, followed by five of the security guards, making the elevator rather crowded.

The remaining seven men stood in the doorway looking at Garret, who in turn looked at his Chief of Security.

'Alissa, your team are awaiting your instructions.' Garret spoke softly and glanced over at the captain.

'This lift wasn't designed for any more people.' The strength of her voice surprised her. 'You seven will remain here. You will stand guard and make sure that no living soul gets past you. We shall remain with the captain and on launch day you will go, as ordered, to the main entrance of the ship. If the mission is successful, we will rendezvous with you there.'

Alissa reached forward to the panel and the door slid shut, sealing the captain with his killer.

***

Shem opened the door. It was the fourth room they had entered on their mission. The room was small and he could see only by the light coming in through the doorway. His eyes flickered around the room as they adjusted to the dark. In the room was a bed, table and chair and a little end table with a lamp. Someone had lived in here. He stepped into the room and walked over to the bed.

'Who do you think lives here?' Ham asked from the doorway.

Shem shrugged. 'No one lives here now.'

Something bothered him though. Standing in this room, looking around, anyone could've lived here, so why was Alissa in his mind? He knew the answer, of course. Alissa was always dancing in the back of his mind. He glanced around one more time, then turned to leave. That's when he stopped short. Turning his head slowly, he looked at the chair. In his entire life, exactly one person had always turned their chair sideways on to a table. It was an uncomfortable and ridiculous thing to do and he mocked her relentlessly for it.

He felt certain, suddenly, that Alissa had been here. They took her here and did something to her. The file he had found detailed a training program for an assassin. Was that her? Had they trained her to kill Captain Andover? Had they taken away his sweet girl and replaced her with something else altogether? He would never forgive them for this. He would destroy whoever did this.

'Shem? What's wrong?' Ham sounded concerned. Slowly his tall companion turned and faced the doorway.

'Nothing's wrong, buddy. Let's keep looking.'
Shem walked out of the room, closing the door behind him. He would have to tell Ham eventually, but not yet, not until he knew more.

They continued on down the hallway, opening doors as they went. Shem was going to bring her back, he was going to save her.

Ham walked in silence. He had sensed the change in Shem's demeanour and knew that something had happened in that room. Shem didn't want to tell him and that was fine. He would confide in him eventually and then the two of them would figure out what to do next, just as they always did. Shem just needed some time, though Ham. And when he needs me, I won't let him down. He fingered the little parcel of green powder in his pocket.

CHAPTER FIFTEEN

THE LIFT DOORS OPENED TO REVEAL A LONG, brightly lit, white metal corridor with a huge steel door at the far end.

The group left the lift and stood awkwardly on the metal flooring. Garret stepped to the front. 'Captain, to get to the bunker we must pass through five doors. Alissa will station one guard at each of them.'

'Okay, that sounds sufficient.'

They walked to the first metal doorway. Garret pressed a button and the door opened. The captain and his son, followed by four guards and Garret, walked through. Alissa turned and rested her hand on the chest of the fifth guard. 'You stay here.' Then she turned and stepped through the doorway into the second corridor. The door slid shut behind them.

'I have programmed a code into this door that only I know.' He
looked at Alissa. 'You will program the next.' She nodded.

They walked to the next door and repeated the process, except this time Alissa programmed the door. She tapped in the first numbers that came to her head, which happened to be Shem's birthday. She surprised even herself with that one.

The group continued onto the next door and Garret programmed a password and they left a man behind.

They passed through the final two doors and left a guard at each of them. They were at the bunker entrance now, just the four of them.

Alissa knew this was the last door and she began to formulate a plan. She needed to be alone in there with the captain – that way she wouldn't have to murder his son. She could tell the boy that the killer waited for them in there, that she had fought bravely beside his father to protect him, but that the killer had gotten the better of her, knocking her unconscious and slaughtering the man she had been charged to protect. As the security chief, they would have to believe her.

Alissa looked over her shoulder at Garret, trying to convey her idea to him, her eyes pleading with him to keep the boy away. Garret returned her gaze but revealed nothing, no little nod to say I understand. Alissa would have to take it on faith that he had read her face.

She turned back to the door and entered the code; the huge metal panel that was the door slid open and the captain stepped inside, followed immediately by Alissa, who turned in the doorway to face Garret. Their eyes met and she prayed silently to herself that this would go smoothly.

Louis tried to sidestep her to get to his father but Garret placed his hand on the boy's shoulder. Louis looked up at the first officer, confused as to why he had stopped him, then his gaze turned to the security chief. Her eyes were cruel and her breath was shallow. She looked evil. Louis realised what was happening but it was too late.

Alissa entered a second code, the door began to slide closed, and that's when everything went into slow motion.

As the door began to close, Alissa looked down at Louis and her arm began to reach for her gun. Louis' eyes widened and he opened his mouth to shout to his father. The sound had barely left his lips before Garret clamped his strong hand over the boy's mouth and lifted him clean off his feet. Garret turned away and the boy's legs kicked violently at the air as the door finally closed.

Alissa's hand found the gun and she whirled round to aim it at the captain when her face exploded in pain and her world went dark.

Garret tossed the boy to the floor and ran to the door panel. He pressed a few keys and the door locked. He turned back to Louis, who sat on the floor in a ball. He walked over and sat beside him.

'One day Louis, you will understand what happened here today. You will never forgive me and I know that, but trust me when I say, I just saved your life.

You will probably spend that life trying to avenge your father and that will be justified. But know this. If we had not completed this mission, every person on the Ark would have been dead before we left the solar system – and I could not allow that to happen.

I will take care of you until launch day. We will remain here. Do you understand?' He looked at the boy and waited. Louis nodded slightly, then rested his head on his arms.

***

Ham and Shem explored the rest of the rooms. They saw training rooms, rooms that looked like medical centres and something that appeared to be a torture device. They had stumbled upon the supply more by accident than design. They had been searching through a room that looked like a schoolroom; it had a little metal table and a chair that was sideways on behind it. Shem's heart sank when he saw it. Alissa had been in here, there was evidence of her everywhere he looked. He knew now that whatever had been done in this facility had been done to her.

Panic started to rise in him. If someone had done all this, gone to so much trouble, where was that someone? That was the thing that was worrying him the most; this place didn't look like it had been empty for long. What if it wasn't? What if there were people watching them, waiting for them? He was becoming paranoid.

As Shem stood in the middle of the room staring at the chair, Ham leant against the wall. It swung in and he toppled backwards into a small closet filled with military apparel. Since then, Shem had been collecting papers and stuffing them into a rucksack he had found in the closet. Ham watched as he did this, mumbling things about proof to himself as they went.

The rucksack was getting heavy now. Shem swapped it from one shoulder to the other. He stopped in one of the hallways and turned to Ham. 'How deep do you think we are?'

'I don't know.'

'Do you remember the map you showed me when we first came in here?'

Ham nodded. He had shown it to Shem but he didn't remember what it said. He'd been on the drugs at the time and they tended to hide things in the back of his mind, just out of reach, until he took them again. He wrapped his fingers gingerly around the little green packet.

'We need to go back to it. I want to see it again. I feel like there is more on the map than there is here. Like something's been blocked off. I want to know what. And why.'

Ham nodded again and relaxed his fingers. He would save the little packet. He didn't need it yet.

***

The four men in black suits stood around their table. In the centre was a screen showing Ham and Shem walking around the facility they had so recently used as a training centre. The two friends wouldn't find them of course. The men were safely hidden away from prying eyes. But what they were seeing was dangerous to the mission.

'Should we kill them?' asked Scar Face.

'It may be our only option,' said Blue Eyes.

'No.'

Three of the men looked at Silver Glove.

'We shall not harm them,' he said.

'I think you will need to elaborate, my friend,' said Blue Eyes, taking a threatening step towards his colleague. Silver Glove stood his ground and refused to blink.

'Alissa is working for us because she believes that doing so will enable her to leave the planet with her friends. If they are dead, she will have no reason to continue. She will not want to live with murder on her conscience if her best friends are not there to help her through it. Trust me. If you kill her friends, we will lose the assassin.'

'It sounds more to me like you want to spare her feelings.' Blue Eyes spat the words at his gloved friend. He was becoming so much more aggressive these days, and the stress of the plan was starting to show. Maybe he wasn't ready for this.

'As always, we shall do whatever it takes to ensure the success of this mission and to protect what is ours. But we will not kill them unless it is completely necessary. Do I make myself clear?'

'Crystal,' was the bitter reply.

***

Alissa sat on the cold metal box and watched her father pulling on the ratchet in the engine of the subway train. It wasn't glamorous but few people could afford the long journey to have him look at their little hovercars, so subway trains became the bulk of his work.

Enoch had grease marks on his face and every time he wiped his forehead he smeared more dirt into his bushy eyebrows. Alissa smiled as she watched her father; he was a good man who had always protected her and taught her well. She had impeccable manners and was often referred to as 'Little Princess' by her dad and his friends.

She stretched her legs out in front of her and rested them on a little tool chest. This was the best way to spend a Saturday.

'Princess? You still over there?' Her dad's deep voice bellowed out of the engine compartment.

'Yeah Dad. Still here.'

'Good. Bring me the laser sealer. Got a hole here big enough to fit a boot through.'

Alissa jumped off the box and grabbed the heavy tool from its place on the shelf. She struggled under the weight as she carried it over to her father. He stood up straight and took the laser from her and smiled as he kissed the top of her forehead. She puffed her chest out, pleased as punch that she had done good for her dad.

'Okay, it's getting late Little Princess, head home now and get yourself cleaned up.'

'But Dad … I want to stay! You're gonna be finished soon and it's not that late!'

'Alissa …' That was his warning voice. If she carried on she'd be grounded and he wouldn't let her come out here with him for weeks.

'It's time to go. Besides, these things are dangerous. If gas leaks into the engine compartment and I turn on the laser—'

'Fine. I'm going.'

She turned and walked towards the door, dragging her feet to make the journey last longer.

'Alissa!' That voice meant business.

'Okay Dad! Bye!' she called as she jogged out the door. As soon as she was out of his view she slowed again. She hated being home alone, but thirteen was too old to cling to your dad all the time. The other kids thought she was weird and had stopped her from hanging out with them years ago.

When she heard the explosion, she turned back to the garage and ran screaming for her father, her face wet with tears, her eyes wild and filled with terror, her arms clawing the air. As she turned the corner she was greeted by a wall of flame …

***

Everything was black. Alissa was becoming aware that she was lying on a cold, hard surface. Her face was burning with pain but she had to help her father. Something was holding her in place, stopping her from getting up. Was she strapped to the bed? Who had done this to her? Then her mind caught up with her and she remembered aiming the gun at the captain. Then...nothing.

The right side of her face was throbbing and her mouth tasted of blood. Opening her eyes she realised something was covering her face.

She had been blinded by the fire. No, that wasn't real. Her brain wasn't ticking like it should be and she felt like she kept missing a beat. Not being able to see was driving her crazy.

Alissa held her breath and listened, but wherever she was, it was silent. She remembered the door closing on Garret and Louis. She remembered grabbing her gun and she remembered turning to shoot the captain. That's when something had hit her. It must've been the captain. He must've heard Louis and realised what was happening.

She tried again to free herself and stand up. Grunting, she struggled against her restraints. This wasn't the plan and it most certainly wasn't fair. Her head started throbbing and she relaxed her muscles and lay silently.

Then she heard footsteps coming towards her. Something grabbed the blindfold and pulled it away from her eyes. Her vision was blurred as she tried to look around. Her body was strapped to a steel surgical bed by harnesses that left very little room to manoeuvre. The locks holding them seemed to be controlled from a panel at the foot of the bed. There was little chance of escape.

The captain, who was now holding the blindfold, sat down on a stool he had placed by her bedside. His face was mere inches from hers; his eyes searched her face for any sign of remorse. There was only confusion. She lay silently, face to face with the man she wanted to kill. She was his prisoner now and would remain here, alone with him, until launch day – unless he killed her.

The captain was the first to speak.

'My son.'

'Safe.' Alissa's throat was dry but she didn't expect that the captain would rush to bring her water.

'You were sent to kill me?'

Alissa stared at the ceiling. She didn't know how much to tell him. Silence filled the room again and she could feel Clarke's anger begin to swell.

'I am the captain! My job is to take responsibility for the lives of every person in my crew and on my ship, to protect them, to help them survive on a new world.'

He rose to his feet. He'd been holding onto this since he found out about the assassin.

'And you have taken it upon yourself to hunt me down and kill me. To leave my son without a father ...' His voice faltered. The thought of leaving Louis was more than he could bear. His breath was ragged. Alissa had never seen someone so angry before.

'Tell me the reason.'

Alissa lay on the bed, staring at the ceiling through swollen eyes, as the captain spoke. Her own voice was croaky from sleep and her swollen lip muffled some of what she was saying, but through gritted teeth she forced the words.

'My mission is to protect the Ark. To stop you from destroying it.'

His expression was almost comical, his mouth open and his eyes wide. He couldn't find the words to express exactly how stupid that sounded.

'What is wrong with you? Do you actually think I want to destroy my ship? That would be suicide, you idiot!'

He rose to his feet. He was astounded by the idea, that much was clear. It confused Alissa; she had become so certain of her mission that trying to defend it seemed silly.

'My son will be on that ship! You think I would kill him?' He was yelling at her now. 'My own son! You're a foolish child!' His words stung her; it was like being yelled at by her own father. 'That really is all you are, isn't it? A child, easily led to believe anything.'

'You're lying.' Her voice was calm. Alissa continued to stare at the ceiling. 'I know the truth Clarke. You lost your wife, your family was broken. It might even have been your own fault. How could you live with that?' Her words were cruel and the captain was reeling from the accusation.

'Someone offered you a way out, didn't they? A way to escape the torture that is your life. All you have to do is take the bomb on board the ship. No one is going to search the captain. You can get anything onto the Ark.'

Clarke still couldn't speak. This girl was insane. But she continued regardless.

'Death kind of messes you up, you know? When you lose someone, someone special...It has a way of changing you. You changed, didn't you?'

The captain stormed to the door of the infirmary and stopped in the doorway. 'I think we should continue this later,' He said. And with that, he switched off the lights and left her alone in the dark.

How had this happened? Trapped in a room with a killer next door. He's going to wait for her to fall asleep and he's going to sneak in and end her.

Alissa needed to escape, and fast, before the captain came back. Her clarity of thought had returned during her argument with Clarke, and she was feeling stronger. Her head still ached and her face was stinging, but at least she was alive.

147

The restraints holding her down crossed over her shoulders, waist and legs. Her feet were tied to the bottom of the bed and her hands were locked in too. She wriggled a bit, trying to loosen the ties. This infirmary hadn't been used in a long time and she hoped that the equipment was old – that way it wouldn't put up much of a fight against her new strength.

She strained against the ties holding her wrists, and the metal started to complain as it bent a fraction. Alissa was using everything she had to pull free. Her head started to pound as the strain pumped blood round her brain, and she started to feel dizzy.

The restraints creaked again as whatever bolted them in place was coming loose. Alissa took a deep breath, gritted her teeth and tensed her arm muscles to the point of breaking. An animalistic growl escaped her lips as she fought her way free and her right arm came free. The sudden release caused her arm to fly upwards, almost hitting Alissa's already broken face. Her newly honed reflexes stopped it just in time.

She rested for a while. The strain of releasing one arm was enough for now; she would try to free her left in a little while.

A small wound on her forehead had opened while she forced her way out of the left restraints, causing blood to trickle into her hair. It had been painful, but both arms were free.

The strap across her shoulders was holding her tightly but if she could manoeuvre it towards her head she might be able to slip under it. Alissa grabbed it and began to push it upwards while sliding herself as far as she could down the metal table. The strap slipped onto her neck and began to tighten again. Her eyes widened as it began to put pressure on her windpipe. It was getting harder to breathe and she couldn't force the strap either way. She was going to die.

Panicking, she tried to call out to the captain. Desperate for help, she flung her arms around, trying to find something to cut the strap with. Her arm connected with the metal stand beside the bed causing it to fall, emptying its contents noisily onto the floor.

Alissa couldn't breathe at all now and little silver spots were dancing in front of her eyes. Her fingers tightened around the straps until her knuckles were white, then they fell limply to her side as her consciousness slipped away.

She felt the pain in her throat before she was fully awake. Alissa could breathe and it felt good to be alive. But this was the second time she had nearly been killed in this place. Maybe she wasn't as prepared as Silver Glove thought.

Opening her eyes she saw Clarke sitting beside the bed looking concerned. Had he saved her? There wasn't really any other explanation. Alissa had certainly not managed to save herself.

She tried sitting up and was surprised to find that the restraints had been released and she was free to move.

'Not having much luck in here are you?'

Clarke's voice was shaky. He had heard the table crash as it fell and figured she'd escaped. He came in ready to take her down again and found the poor girl with her eyes rolled back in her head and not breathing. If she died he would have no way of figuring out who was behind all of this.

'You saved my life,' Alissa croaked.

'It's nothing personal. I need you alive.'

Alissa furrowed her brow. 'I don't understand.' She looked around
the room. It was a bit of a mess for a medical facility. There was broken glass around her bed and a rather large streak of blood leading from the door, from when the captain had dragged her in here. She looked back at Clarke. 'I have to know the truth; I have some questions for you. Will you answer them?'

He lifted his head and looked at her. 'Ask away.'

'Okay, Captain. Arks have left this planet every two years for a decade. What happened to those Arks?'

'They each took a different course in search of a New World.'

'I thought a world had already been found?'

'That was a lie, told by the government to stop the people of Earth from panicking. The Arks' true mission has been to find a home for the human race.'

'But none of the Arks ever made it out of the solar system. Each captain was charged with an assignment. Destroy the Ark to prevent humans from surviving. That was your mission; it has been the mission of every captain for the last ten years. I have to stop you.'

Alissa felt uncomfortable: it was truly a bizarre and unlikely situation. Here they sat, assassin and target, discussing the reasons behind their actions. No amount of training could have prepared the socially awkward Alissa Namaah for this.

The captain spoke evenly. 'My mission has always been, and will always be, to protect the passengers and crew on my ship. No Arks have ever been destroyed and I don't know where you got your information—'

'Captain, I've seen it.' Alissa rose to her feet, carefully avoiding the broken glass. 'Garret found the footage. It's over, we know the truth.'

'What footage?'

The captain was clearly being difficult. He knew the truth; why did she have to spell it out for him?

'Garret found footage from one of the orbiting satellites that shows every single Ark being destroyed as it leaves Earth. I was told about your mission by the men in the black suits. They know about you and they want to protect humanity. They trained me for this.'

'You're wrong.' It was the Captain's turn to stand up. He was at least six inches taller than her and his voice rose with his conviction.

'The Arks are out there, they're searching for a new world, and we're going to join them in their search.'

'You really believe that, don't you?'

He nodded. She had never seen such sincerity in anyone other than Ham.

'I don't understand …' She sounded younger than she had in a long time. Her hand came up to her face and she gingerly touched the welt on her cheek. It was sore and caked with dry blood. She flinched as she pressed on a particularly tender part and her eyes began to water.

Her swollen lip was aching from all the talking. She was beginning to feel very sorry for herself.

The captain walked over to the sink and started soaking rags.

'This is going to sting – quite a bit actually.'

He smiled at her as she silently watched him walk back over to the bedside with a wet cloth, a bowl of clean water and some spray she didn't recognise. He encouraged her to sit back on the bed and she raised her knees up and leaned on her elbows. Clarke gently pressed the wet cloth against her cheek, and the pain surged through her whole face. She had a broken cheekbone; that much was evident.

'What did you hit me with?' Alissa flinched away from his touch.

The captain looked a little sheepish. 'A chair.'

'You hit me in the head with a chair?'

'You wanted to kill me.'

The silence that followed was awkward indeed. Theirs was going to be an unusual relationship. She couldn't kill the captain until she knew the truth and Clarke needed to find out for himself what was going on.

The captain rinsed the cloth and began cleaning away the dried blood from her face. There was an understanding between them. It was unspoken but they both knew that neither would kill the other. Not now at least. Not until they were free of the bunker.

'Captain—'

'Call me Clarke, that's my name.'

'Okay, Clarke. Garret isn't going to hurt your son.'

The captain's jaw tightened. 'I know.'

'I thought I would have to kill him.' She looked him in the eyes. 'I was ready to kill him.'

Her expression hadn't changed but the captain's had. She was a monster after all. The men that did this to her took away all of her innocence.

The captain silently cleaned her face and picked up the spray.

Alissa looked at it; she had never seen anything like it before. 'What is that stuff?'

'It's going to heal your wounds. It will repair your bones, seal your skin and reduce the swelling.'

'Will it hurt?'

'No, of course not.'

The captain sprayed the side of her face and it felt like a thousand searing hot knives were slowly breaking her skin and slicing her face open bit by bit. She gritted her teeth through the pain but that made it feel worse.

'Liar!'

'Relax, Alissa, you have to relax. It's supposed to be quite painful but trust me, it works.' He raised his shirt to reveal a small scar on his ribcage. She looked at it through watery eyes. The pain was constant and getting worse. She relaxed her whole face but nothing brought relief.

'Focus Alissa. Look at me. I was shot in an accident during a battle simulation. It broke all the ribs on my left side, punctured my lung.'

Alissa's eyes began to roll into the back of her head. 'Look at me! Focus.' His hands were on her shoulders now, his voice loud enough to echo through the pain.

'It blasted out my back and took a good chunk of me with it. This stuff saved my life.' She tried to focus on him but the knives felt like they were getting deeper, they were going to pierce into her skull and mash up her brain. Then it stopped getting worse.

It reached its peak and began slowly to subside. Her breathing began to slow and she stopped shaking. The captain helped her lie down. Her face was beginning to feel numb. 'Water,' she croaked.

The captain smiled and walked over to the sink. He grabbed a glass and filled it. By the time he got back to her bedside the pain had subsided, replaced by a feeling of pins and needles. It felt like all the bones in her face had splintered and now the little shards were poking into her skin from the inside. She raised herself onto her elbows and drank deeply from the water that the captain handed her.

When she had drained the glass she lay back down. She was exhausted.

'The drowsiness is a side effect of the spray. Your body needs to rest to fully heal itself. Get some sleep now and I'll see you in the morning.'

With that Alissa's eyes closed and everything went black for a third time.

***

Garret sat on the floor outside the bunker, listening. There was no sound from inside, but then the door was a foot thick so he didn't expect to hear anything. He wanted to open the door, to free Alissa from the Hell she must be enduring, sharing living quarters with a corpse. He was horrified by the thought.

The boy had disappeared a while ago. The outer shell of the bunker was a giant ring, a huge corridor full of nooks and crannies.

No doubt he was looking for a way in, to try to save his father, but he would be back soon enough. The only food dispenser in this entire section of the complex was right beside where Garret was sitting.

He knew that if the child realised it, he would be able to reprogram the machine to feed him any number of toxic substances disguised as real food, or he could stop it from working altogether and starve the first officer until he agreed to free them.

Garret would have to try to make the child understand the truth about his father. He was a terrorist and he needed to be stopped. Garret was the good guy in all of this and poor Louis was just caught in the crossfire.

The child came around the bunker and sat down on the floor opposite Garret.

'Tell me how to get into the bunker.'

The child was definitely brave. Not like me, thought Garret. As a child, I was scared of my own reflection, living in my father's shadow because it was safer than being my own man. The realisation made Garret feel sick. He was angry at the child for being defiant and for reminding Garret of his own shortcomings.

'Your father is dead.' Garret realised his mistake the moment the words left his mouth, but it was too late now. He braced himself for the inevitable tears, but nothing happened. The boy's shoulders sagged and for the first time he looked like he really believed it.

Was there a hint of relief? Garret shook his head to rid himself of such a ridiculous idea.

'Who will take care of me?' Louis sounded so young.

'We'll find you a foster family on board the Ark. You won't be

alone.'

'This is your fault.'

'I know. It's late now. Go to sleep. There are bunks through the

door to your left.'

Louis obediently got to his feet and walked through the door. Garret followed him and locked the door. He would feel safer knowing that the child wouldn't slit his throat while he slept. He walked back to the dispenser and sat beneath it. He closed his eyes and drifted off to sleep.

***

Ham and Shem had finally arrived back at the map room and were copying the map onto paper. Shem knew it had gotten late but he wasn't ready to stop yet. He hadn't slept properly in days and he had only eaten things they had found on their search. He was running on adrenaline and his body was getting ready to crash on him.

The map itself showed all the rooms he had investigated, and more. It turned out that he and Ham were a lot deeper that he first thought and they could go deeper still if they wanted to. There were stairs and tunnels leading much further underground. The level they had been searching was bigger than he realised too. There seemed to be hidden doors throughout the entire system, doors leading to more hallways that would always seem to circle round and meet other hidden doors.

It was more that Shem could handle. His eyes started to droop and he began to feel exhaustion overtake him.

The underground facility stretched under the whole of New Amerland and it was layer upon layer of secret rooms. He knew now that they would never search them all; it would take weeks to explore every room. They had to be smart about this. They had to figure out which room would hold the information they needed, then use it to find out what had happened to Alissa down here, and where they could find her.

Ham was good at drawing; he enjoyed sketching the map while Shem pointed at things and grew increasingly frustrated. He was tired though, and hungry.

'Shem, it's time to sleep now.' Ham had stopped drawing and was looking at his friend.

'We can't stop now, we have to find out—'

'No Shem, it's time to sleep now.'

Shem sat down on a chair and rested his head on the table. Within seconds he was fast asleep.

LAUNCH MINUS FOUR

CHAPTER SIXTEEN

ALISSA'S EYES SLOWLY OPENED. THE ROOM CAME into focus and she realised she was still in the infirmary. She slowly sat up and looked around. The broken glass from the night before had been cleaned up but the blood stain was still there. It sent a shudder up her spine to think how differently this could've gone.

Her hand made its way to her face and she realised that there was no pain. The spray had definitely done what it was supposed to do. So far as she could tell she was fully healed.

'Amazing stuff,' she said to herself.

Alissa edged her way off the bed and onto her bare feet. She felt steadier than she had yesterday and she knew that whatever concussion she had must've been taken care of by the spray.

The infirmary was huge; there were steel beds like the one she had slept on, metal cabinets filled with medicines and supplies, small metal stools and shelves upon shelves of sterilised, vacuum-packed medical equipment. The bunker itself was massive. The entrance hall, where she had been knocked unconscious, led to the medi-bay if you went left and the captain's quarters if you headed to the right.

Alissa thought about the situation she had landed herself in. She was trapped in a protected bunker, miles underground with the man she was supposed to assassinate – who had tried to kill her and then saved her life and treated her injuries. It wasn't a desirable situation or one anyone could've predicted. She had to find a way out.

The things the captain had told her confused her mission. She wasn't sure what the truth was anymore. The worst part was, she didn't know if she could trust the man with the silver glove. He had made her strong and protected her from the worst excesses of the others. He cared for her, she knew that; so who was lying? None of it made any sense to her.

While she was looking around the infirmary for anything she could make use of, the captain walked in. He stood watching her as she rooted through cabinets. He caught himself smiling, then quickly frowned. This girl was trying to kill him, and he shouldn't need to be reminded of that. He coughed to announce his arrival and Alissa stopped what she was doing and turned to face him.

The awkwardness between them wouldn't ever go away. She looked down at the floor.

'How are you feeling this morning?' He sounded genuinely concerned.

'I'm fine. The pain is gone. I'm worried though.' She walked over to the steel table and used is as a seat. 'We're trapped in here, and we are going to continue being trapped until Garret lets us out on launch day, and by then it'll be too late.'

'What will be too late?' The captain's voice was calm.

'Something is destroying the Arks. I've seen it. And if you're telling me that it's not you – and I'm still not sure I believe you – but if it's not, then...' She paused, trying to figure out if she should tell him. 'If it's not, something else is going to destroy that ship in four days, and we have to stop it.'

'And that means escaping the bunker.'

'Yeah. But this place is sealed for your safety.' Something about that phrase struck Alissa as hilarious and she burst out laughing. The captain stared at her as the corners of his own mouth started to curve. He didn't fight it and instead joined her in her amusement.

***

Ham nudged Shem's shoulder, gently at first but then harder and harder until Shem's eyes flew open.

'Ham!' Shem sat bolt upright. His friend was looking at him and smiling.

'Good morning, buddy!' Ham was unusually cheery for someone who had slept on a metal floor deep underground.

'Why're you so happy?'

Ham, still smiling, pushed a bowl under his grumpy friend's nose.

Shem's eyes widened as he inhaled. 'That smells amazing, what is it?'

'It's chicken soup.'

'But there is no meat anymore. How is there chicken soup?'

'I don't know. I found a storage area down the hall. It's full of fresh food and supplies.'

'How do we know it's safe?'

Ham's face crumpled up as he thought about it. 'I guess we don't. But if we don't eat then we'll starve, and if we starve we can't save Alissa.'

Ham's logic was simple yet flawless.

'Fair enough.' Shem lifted the soup to his lips and slurped from the bowl. His eyes closed as he ate and the soup tasted glorious, like nothing he had ever tasted before.

Shem wanted to savour every mouthful, let it sit on his tongue and excite his senses. But before he knew it the soup was gone. He was satisfied. His eyes followed the empty bowl as he tried to put it down on the table. But his arms wouldn't work like he wanted them to. They felt cumbersome and not his own. His eyelids were becoming heavy and he struggled to keep them open.

Shem's happiness ebbed away and was quickly replaced with fear. Everything around him seemed fuzzy and thick, he looked around for Ham and spotted him kneeling on the ground, his eyes half-closed, showing just the whites. Shem watched in horror as his friend rocked back and forth slightly before he fell forwards, his face meeting the floor with a smack.

Shem reached out his hands to his best friend. He needed to make sure Ham was okay. He wanted to stand up but his legs felt like they were made of lead. He tried desperately to stay awake. He concentrated on Alissa. She gave him strength, and his hands slammed onto the table as he pushed himself to his feet. The triumph he felt lasted only a second before his legs gave way and he collapsed into an unconscious heap on the floor.

**

Garret stared at the door and it genuinely felt like it was staring back at him. He would have to open it soon and let the boy out. But what would happen then? What would Garret find?

He'd probably find exactly what he deserved, a vicious end brought about by a vengeful child. Why was he so paranoid these days?

The boy made Garret feel uneasy, but for reasons he couldn't
describe. The files he'd been given talked about the captain killing his wife and son, but Louis was here, plain as day and as real as any of them. The files were obviously wrong about that. That's how the seeds of doubt are sown, and Garret couldn't shake the feeling that something wasn't right. A man had been condemned to death by people he'd never met and here was Garret, ensuring it actually happened.

Garret regretted falling asleep; his mind was always working overtime but never so much as when he first woke up. His bones creaked audibly as he rose painfully to his feet. Sleeping on a metal floor was not good for him – he was an old man. Tonight he would share the bunk with the boy.

Garret stretched his arms and yawned, deciding to get some breakfast from the dispenser and take it to the boy. Maybe they could talk more over food. Fake bacon and toast seemed like a good choice – it was, after all, a favourite of his and he'd never met a soul on this Earth who didn't like Fake Bacon.

The hot food slid into the opening and Garret picked up the tray, walked with it over to the locked door and hit the buttons a few times until the door opened with a whoosh. He stepped inside and looked around. His face fell and the tray slipped out of his grasp and crashed onto the floor. The boy was gone.

CHAPTER SEVENTEEN

'CAPTAIN! COME AND LOOK AT THIS!' ALISSA'S clothes had been cleaned by the Wall-Hole and she was fully dressed, staring at the wall above the bed. Her hair was tied in a knot on the top of her head, still slightly wet from the shower she had taken earlier that morning.

Alissa listened for the sound of his footsteps while continuing to stare. The captain walked in and looked at her.

'What've you found?'

'It's a hatchway, probably from when they were building the place. It may be a way out.'

'Great! Let's get it open then!'

'Yeah, only we need tools to do that and there is nothing in here except food and medical supplies.'

The captain looked around the room to see if anything would be of use. He grabbed a torch and the healing spray and put them in his pocket. *You never know*, he thought. He looked at this girl, so young, and wondered if he was about the do the right thing.

Escaping with her was putting an awful lot on the line but he knew that he would need her – if he could keep her on his side.

'Alissa...'

His voice trailed off as she turned to look at him. His hand was outstretched, showing her what he had found. A smile widened as she looked at what he was holding. There was no way he could be serious, and her eyes met his as she tried to read his intentions. Clarke Andover gave no clues in the way he looked at her, so she reached out and took from his grasp her holster with two guns, and the long serrated knife that usually lived in her boot.

Now she had a sense of normality, which was ironic as before all of this started she had abhorred violence and weaponry of any kind.

Alissa clipped the belt round her waist, tucked the knife away and in one fluid movement she had taken a gun from its holster, armed it and aimed it at the hatchway. Alissa Namaah was good and the captain knew it. His eyes were locked on her face as she pointed the weapon.

But then her face changed. Clarke frowned and followed her gaze. The hatch was gone, leaving behind a hole large enough for the two of them to climb through.

'How did that happen?'

'I don't know. It just ... vanished.' Alissa was still staring at the opening while the captain walked over to one of the metal beds. He started to push it towards her but even with all of his strength he was unable to move it more than a couple of inches. Alissa realised what he was doing and walked over to him. Standing beside him she began to push the bed as well. By their combined effort, the heavy bed slowly scratched along the floor. It was energy-draining work but eventually the bed stopped right underneath their escape route.

The captain jumped onto the bed and grabbed the torch out of his pocket. When he stood up straight his head and shoulders disappeared through the opening. He was quiet for a few minutes and Alissa watched the light flashing around and waited patiently for his report.

'It looks like an air vent. It's dusty and quite horrible but there is enough space to crawl through here. I think this our best option.' His voice echoed as he spoke. Alissa watched as he gripped the edges of the opening and pulled himself up. He disappeared completely.

'Captain?'

'Yeah, I'm still here. Come on up.'

Alissa climbed onto the bed but was shorter than the captain and couldn't quite reach the edges. She jumped up and grabbed on and used her momentum to carry her legs up. Her feet swung into the vent and she followed through with her upper body. The captain looked impressed.

Alissa surveyed her surroundings. It was indeed filthy in the vent and it smelled of damp, but there was enough room to comfortably crawl one behind the other.

They set off to find a way out. The captain was in front with the torch, and every time they moved they stirred up a cloud of dust that enveloped them, causing them to cough and sneeze.

They followed the crawl space for what seemed like hours. Every few minutes the captain would shout back to Alissa to make sure she was okay, and she found herself thinking about their time in the bunker. The captain had certainly been kind to her, healed her wounds, and she had done nothing in return. She realised that the captain was taking an awful lot on faith.

***

'They have escaped.'

Silver Glove looked at the screen his comrade was monitoring. He saw Alissa and the captain crawl through the hole in the ceiling. He smiled.

'Good.'

The man with the tattoo walked up to the screen.

'I don't understand. Why are we allowing them to leave?' His voice was dripping with resentment. Silver Glove turned slowly to face him, looking silently into his friend's eyes.

'I'm going to explain this to you but I'm only going to explain it once so I hope you're listening closely. The assassin and the captain were talking, she was beginning to question us. If we had left them alone together in there, they would inevitably have come to the same conclusion and that conclusion would have been that we are the enemy. Now you know the training that she has had and you understand exactly what she is capable of. Do you want her to turn her newfound abilities on you? Who will complete the mission if we're no longer here? We need to see this through to the end no matter what.'

The one with the tattoo held Silver Glove's gaze for a few moments before he turned and walked away. Silver Glove turned his attention back to the monitor. Blue Eyes was still standing next to him. 'How do we get her to complete her mission,' he said.

Silver Glove stared, unblinking, at the monitor.

'We don't give her a choice. Her mind is clouded by the captain and we need to give her clarity. We will bring her friends here. She will come for them and I expect the captain will come with her. That will give her the perfect opportunity to complete the job and remember, they must not find the boy. We will draw them to us.'

'And what happens to us when she gets here?'

Blue Eyes had a point and Silver Glove turned to face him. 'We must do as commanded.'

Silver Glove looked longingly at the screen where Alissa had previously been.

'If she completes the mission then it doesn't matter what she does to us.'

CHAPTER EIGHTEEN

GARRET WAS TRAPPED. THAT WAS THE BASIC TRUTH of this situation. Garret was trapped with no escape. *Calm down Garret*! He instructed. It was clear the boy had disappeared, but how? If he raised the alarm they'd both be court martialled for treason, and in his long life Garret had seen people executed for less.

The outright murder of a captain was unthinkable. And he'd been a party to it, in fact the whole plan was his idea. Garret took deep breaths, tried to calm himself. His options were definitely limited.

He walked into the room where Louis was last seen. Garret's hands searched all around the walls, feeling for hidden panels or doors. He stood on the bunk and felt the ceiling, and he knelt on the floor, knees creaking in protest as he checked for escape routes. He stopped and surveyed the room. This was bad. There was no way the kid could've gotten out. How did he do it?

Garret slowly got onto his feet and walked back into the main hallway. He looked at the bunker door. Was the captain dead yet? Was it worth opening the door and letting them out? That decision was not his to make and for the first time in many years he was feeling something other than disdain for all those around him.

He worried about Alissa. She was only a child after all, and Garret had allowed her to give in to her darker inclinations; he'd encouraged it and he'd helped her become a murderer. Suddenly he was full of regret, and the heaviness of his heart was enough to make him realise that he should have done it himself. The captain should've been his target.

A plan of action was required here – moping around in this hallway wasn't helping. Garret ran his fingers through his thinning hair and stood up straight. He walked over to the bunker door.

***

Ham's eyes cracked open and stung as they filled with light. They were dry and sore and it was an effort just to keep them open, he was so tired. Looking around the room, he thought everything looked strange. And something was missing.

He was lying on the floor, with no recollection of how he got there. Casting his mind back, he remembered eating soup with Shem, and then nothing. He must've rolled around on the floor while he was out because now he was curled up in the corner under a table.

Ham saw Shem lying in the middle of the room and frowned at his sleeping friend. He decided to wake him up but no sound came out of his mouth. Ham was scared now; why couldn't he say anything? He tried to crawl over to Shem but he couldn't move either. Ham was completely helpless – all he could do was lie there and cry like a baby.

Then Ham heard footsteps, getting closer to the room and accompanied by voices, too. Panic started to set in. He wanted to grab his friend and drag him out of the way to safety, hide him, but he couldn't. Even with a body full of adrenaline, whatever was keeping him paralysed wasn't wearing off. All he could do was watch as the door opened and four men in black suits walked in.

The one in front was tall with dark hair. He looked scary and he had a glove that looked like solid silver. Ham didn't like him. The man was looking at something and when Ham followed his gaze, he realised that the man was looking at Shem. The man with the silver glove took a few steps closer and crouched down beside Ham's best friend.

'What's this?' he asked in a playful voice. 'How did you get in here? And where's your fat friend?' His eyes narrowed and he scanned the room for Ham. His eyes flittered around the spot where Ham was but he must have been well hidden because he looked right past him and back to Shem.

'All alone are we?' Silver Glove grinned as he stood up, looked at two of his companions and nodded. Ham's eyes filled with tears as they grabbed Shem and began to drag him to the door.

That's when Ham noticed it. Something about these four men was off. Something wasn't right and Ham knew what it was. The 'fat friend' lay there with his new knowledge and waited.

***

The captain looked at the grille at the end of the crawl space. It was securely bolted and prevented an easy exit. He shouldered it hard in a vain effort to force it free. He was angry and Alissa could feel it radiating from him. 'Goddammit!'

His voice echoed through the metallic crawl space as Alissa sat in silence. If this was going to be his breakdown he needed to get it out of his system now because she needed him clear-minded and focused.

An awkward silence fell between them and neither could face breaking it. The captain slammed his hands against the grimy panel and grunted as he did so. This wasn't just about a barrier to him – they both knew that Alissa could free them – this was about his son.

The captain rubbed his eyes with his thumb and forefinger and choked back a ragged sob of sheer frustration.

Alissa reached out to him and placed her hand on his shoulder.

'That's enough now, Clarke.'

Her voice was gentle and the captain felt it wrap around him protectively. He turned in the small space to look at her filthy face and noticed some of her hair had tumbled out of the knot and was clinging to the combination of sweat and dirt caked on her face and neck.

She smiled sympathetically at Clarke and it pained him. How had he become this man, this man that needed the pity of his own assassin.

The captain had never been this man before. His train of thought took him back to his early thirties, newly wed to the woman of his dreams. They had their whole lives ahead of them., blissful years that passed all too quickly; and in time they had a beautiful son.

Louis was the perfect child and he completed their perfect family. Clarke was the brave starship captain and she was the beautiful technician. They travelled the solar system together in various crafts, exploring their surrounding planets and mining what they could.

Clarke's memory was rose-tinted, of course, but that didn't stop him from missing her terribly. He remembered the day she announced her latest assignment. A little ship called The Hawk. It was an exploratory mission to the furthest reaches of the solar system. It would've been a yearlong assignment and it was going to be the longest they'd ever been apart.

'I can open the hatch.'

Her voice snapped him back to the present. He focused his gaze on Alissa. She was so young – too young for a weight like this on her shoulders. Clarke reached out to her and wiped some of the dirt from her forehead and in return Alissa offered him a sympathetic smile.

'Swap places with me.'

It was a tight squeeze but they managed to shuffle past each other with only one moment of awkwardness. Their faces were so close and if it was anyone else it might have ended differently. It lasted a second longer than it should have, and they both knew it.

The captain backed away from the panel and Alissa took position in front of it. She was sitting on her lower back using her arms to hold herself steady. She raised her knees to her chest, shuffled forward and rested her feet on the panel. She took one deep breath and on the exhale she thrust her legs out, breaking the panel and sending it flying.

She slid forward and jumped down to the hallway below. Landing elegantly in a crouch, Alissa stood and looked around. The hallway was completely deserted so she took a few steps back and looked up at the hole in the wall as the captain dropped out. They stood in silence for a moment. Nothing was holding them together now, there was no escape to make, no life to save, nothing stopping Alissa from pulling her gun and ending this now.

'I have to find my son.' The captain's face was set in determination as he broke the silence and set off jogging down the hallway. Alissa stood there staring at him as he moved further and further away; that had taken her by surprise, she'd expected a conversation, perhaps even an argument about what to do next. But Clarke had obviously decided to do this right from the start.

Alissa knew that she had to stick with him – he was still a potential target. Her feet pounded the hallway floor as she chased after her captain.

CHAPTER NINTEEN

EVERYTHING HURTS. THAT WAS THE ONLY THING in Shem's mind as the fog in his brain slowly started to clear. There was something wrapped around his head, covering his eyes, and he could feel that he was tied up. His wrists had been strapped together and tied above his head. His feet were only just touching the floor. The pain was excruciating and his shoulders screamed their protest. How could he think through this?

Suddenly he thought of Ham. Where was he? He shifted fractionally, and cried out in pain.

'Ham?' Shem's voice came out horse and quiet. He cleared his throat and tried again. 'Ham!' Clearer and louder this time. 'Where are you?'

'He's not here.'

Shem froze. He didn't recognise the voice and he felt a hand on his head and the blindfold was pulled away roughly. It took quite a few hairs with it, causing Shem to grunt in pain and open his eyes.

The room wa a large space with white tile walls, floor and ceiling. There were florescent lights in the ceiling which made his eyes ache and his head throb.

Though half-closed eyes Shem could see three men sitting round a table in the centre of the room. Something on the screen built into the table had their attention. The fourth man was standing right in front of him holding the blindfold in his silver glove.

'Who are you people?'

Silver Glove smiled at his captive.

'That information is way beyond your security clearance my
friend.'

'Why am I here?'

'You're here because we need you to be here. Your presence will lure the assassin. She is the key player in all of this. You're the bait.'

The realisation hit Shem hard. His best friend, that's who he was talking about – the gentle, kind and clumsy girl that he had loved from the moment he met her. She was the assassin.

'What have you done to her?'

'We made her strong, fast and...deadly. And if by some miracle you manage to get out of here alive, you'd do well to remember that.'

It was an ominous warning that predicted all sorts of trouble in Shem's future. Assuming, of course, that he had one.

Silver Glove turned to join his companions studying the screen.

***

Ham's legs were shaky. He grabbed the edge of the table and let it take his weight as he pulled himself up off the floor. He was standing when the table finally gave up the fight and toppled onto its side, taking Ham with it.

He had been here for hours, just lying and waiting for his body to cooperate with his requests. Ham knew that he needed to get up because he knew who the shadowy men were now – he had to find Alissa and tell her.

Ham rolled onto his hands and pushed himself up onto his knees. He stopped on all fours, panting like a dog. But he had to keep going now. He continued to fight gravity and eventually pushed his way onto his feet with much straining and some choice words. His breath was coming in jagged rasps and while his legs felt like jelly, his muscles were beginning to function properly again.

The large man used the wall to balance himself and looked around the room. He spotted the rucksack Shem had been carrying, on the floor beneath the table, and smiled to no one but himself.

Walking across the room gave Ham's legs some much needed practice and once at the table, he reached down and plucked the rucksack off the floor. He opened the flap and emptied the contents onto the table, causing papers to float gently to his feet; he rifled through the papers that remained and grabbed one in particular. In scruffy handwriting on a dirty piece of scrap paper was the map he had drawn for Shem. As he looked at it, his brow furrowed with concentration. It was difficult to understand all the little lines and squares that made up a surprisingly accurate picture of the facility.

At first he couldn't figure out where he was on the map, but eventually his eyes lit up and he stuffed everything back into the rucksack except for the map itself, which he held tightly in his hand. He had decided to get back to the map room and establish his current location. From there it would be easy to figure out the quickest way back to the complex.

Ham half-walked, half-ran to the door he'd watched Shem being dragged through, and opened it. He was hoping that it'd been long enough since the men had been around and that his presence would still be unnoticed. Ham had to get back up to the main levels and find Alissa. He ran as fast as he could through the facility, praying that it wasn't too late to save his friends, fortunately finding the map room turned out to be easier than he had first suspected.

When he reached the little room with the map on the wall he was exhausted. He was a big man and running even that short distance was tough. Sweat was dripping into his eyes, making the map on the wall almost unreadable.

Ham was struggling anyway and the more his mind failed him the more he panicked. His breathing was heavy as he recovered from the run that got him here and he had hoped that seeing the map on the wall would help him understand the paper in his hand. The excitement that came with that idea had thoroughly died down now.

Ham's fingers trailed along the surface of the map. It was smooth, made of some sort of clear plastic with the lines that made up the hallways and rooms colour coded to some sequence he couldn't comprehend. He traced the lines until he found the little room that he was in, then with his other hand he slowly worked along the outer edges of the map looking for exits.

His fingers stopped on a doorway that was close enough to where he was, and by moving his hands towards each other, following the green line, he finally brought them together. That was his escape.

He used a damp sleeve to wipe away the worst of the sweat that had built up on his brow, and he concentrated on the little green line. His eyes followed the route he needed to take, over and over again.

Grabbing a pen from the table, Ham drew a line on his paper scrawl to show him where he needed to go.

Straight out the door – left – left – straight – right – straight – left again – and there would be a door on the right that would lead him out of the underground facility. He walked out of the door and started on his way.

CHAPTER TWENTY

'OKAY CAPTAIN, THAT'S ENOUGH!' ALISSA'S VOICE was loud in an otherwise silent stretch of corridor.

Clarke stopped and turned slowly to face her. He look surprised, like he'd forgotten that she was following him. Alissa's face was set in determination, and in that moment Clarke's heart broke for the child. This whole endeavour had aged this poor girl, turned her into something dark and cruel.

'We can't chase around looking for your son. He is with Garret and he is safe. You have my word.'

Her words were chosen carefully and spoken slowly, and with authority. Alissa began to walk towards the captain. 'Right now we have bigger problems. The men that set my mission will be watching me. They'll want to know when you're dead and I can't think straight.

But I think you'll agree that we need to find the truth in all of this.'

'ALISSA ... NAMAAH.'

Alissa whirled around to look at the monitor in the wall. Beside it a terminal whirred into life and the screen flickered reveal Silver

Glove's smiling face.

Clarke stared at the man. With his dark hair and hard features he was terrifying to look at, yet he couldn't tear his eyes away.

Alissa's heart jumped. She would never be able to explain the attraction that she felt for her kidnapper, but the feeling made her euphoric, her breath catching in her throat as she gazed upon his beautiful face. Alissa knew from her conversations with the captain that something wasn't right with this whole situation but when faced with the man in the silver glove, she had a desperate need to make him happy. This wasn't the woman she'd grown to be, so what was happening to her?

'I have something of yours.' Silver Glove's voice scratched into her consciousness and Alissa watched as his smile grew into something closer to a snarl. Alissa gasped in horror as he stepped to one side to reveal Shem. How dare he touch Shem. No matter what her feelings were for Silver Glove, she would slaughter him if he hurt her best friend.

The captain stepped beside her and rested his hand on her shoulder. Alissa felt the slight pressure from his hand and straightened up, looking Silver Glove in the eye and speaking with calm deliberation.

'Let him go.' Her face was hardening. Silver Glove had made her angry, but it was a contained and single-minded anger.

'Come and get him Alissa.'

With that the screen went black. Alissa stood staring at the spot where Shem had been. Her eyes threatened tears but she wouldn't let them fall. She, Alissa Namaah, was stronger than this now. She slammed her fist down hard into the panel, releasing her frustration and shattering the display, causing the machine to go into shutdown.

No words would make this easier and Clarke knew that. Shem's life was in grave danger and Alissa must surely believe what Clarke had been saying all along. Why would the men do this? It was a risky move.

'Where were they?' The captain's voice echoed in Alissa's ears.

'I don't know.' She still hadn't blinked.

'Yes you do. They wouldn't take him somewhere that you've never been. You have to know where they are.'

The captain had a point. Alissa's eyes dropped to the floor while she thought. The only place she'd ever seen them was the underground facility – and once in the hall outside Shem's apartment. They could be anywhere. Alissa couldn't decide. She focused on the essentials.

They had Shem. She needed him to be okay. They couldn't be allowed to keep him. If Clarke Andover was what they wanted then that's exactly what they'd get.

'Alissa.'

She looked up at the captain, and her runaway thoughts stopped in their tracks. Alissa wished this would all go away – the mission, the men, the Ark – she wished she was back at the garage again, fixing ships with Ham. She wished she was at Saime's drinking the poverty away with Shem.

Shem.

'Come on. Think.' Clarke's voice interrupted her again.

'They'll be in the facility. It's under the city. They'll be hidden away so no one will find them. I know how to get there.'

Alissa turned in the direction they needed to go, and called to the captain over her shoulder.

'I need you to come with me.'

***

Ham stood in a tiny room. It was barely three feet square and his ample frame took up most of it. The map had led him through a maze of corridors to this little room. The walls were bare brick, something people in the complex hadn't seen in a long time.

Ham studied the ladder – helpfully attached to the wall opposite – that would aid his escape. Well Mr Ladder, here we are. I'm going to beat you, so just behave yourself, okay?

Ham's eyes followed the metal frame upwards and realised just how far he had to go to reach the hatch. It could easily be three, maybe four floors. It was a long way to go for someone as unfit as Ham and the fear began to creep into his mind – little green tendrils, it seemed to him, wrapping themselves around his pink, squishy brain. It would stop him if he let it, and then Shem would die, Alissa would be lost forever and he would be alone.

Ham took a deep breath, grabbed the rungs just above his head and began to pull himself upwards...

Four levels above, a hatchway in the corridor lifted to reveal Ham's round face. The journey up had been surprisingly easy. In his mind he had held pictures of Shem and Alissa, and his desire to save them had kept him going long after he should've quit.

Ham pushed the hatch all the way open and heaved his bulk through. As he looked around to get his bearings he noticed the grated floor and grey metal wall. He was close to Saimes' Bar, maybe a five minute walk if you weren't in a hurry. His feet started running towards the garages before Ham had even decided to go. His body was on autopilot now, working just ahead of his own slow thoughts.

Excitement pulsed through his veins as he thought about what he needed to do. 'Ham is a man with a plan,' he said under his breath.

The corner that nearly caused him to collide at full speed with a little boy was exactly the same as all the other corners in the complex at this hour – people just weren't around. Ham never expected to see the kid and was horrified at the thought of ploughing through him.

Ham tried to apply the brakes and the momentum he had built up carried him over his now stationary feet and he toppled to the ground, landing heavily. The little boy just watched as the big man sprawled in front of him.

Ham pushed himself to his feet, gulping down huge breaths and dripping with sweat. He was annoyed with himself but he turned his annoyance on the child.

'Why are you just standin' there, kid?'

Louis cocked his head to the side.

'Why are you running?'

Ham looked at the boy. His temper, which only rose when he was hurt or embarrassed, was subsiding.

'I was...I've gotta go to the garage.'

'Why?'

'I've got to help my friend.'

'I don't have any friends.' Louis looked sheepishly at the floor.

With that confession Ham's mood changed completely. He felt sorry for the boy. He could relate because when he was younger, Ham was the one without any friends. The sting of loneliness had stayed with Ham right into adulthood.

'I'll be your friend. My name's Ham.'

'I'm Louis. If you're my friend, will you help me find my house? I'm lost.'

Ham looked around. He needed to go to the garage as quickly as possible and this kid could live anywhere. He frowned and looked down at Louis.

'I know where you live, follow me.' Ham turned and started walking down the corridor, and the kid followed him.

***

Old fingers danced over the locking panel for the bunker and Garret couldn't bring himself to unlock the door. He'd been waiting for something but he didn't know what. Maybe a sign from Alissa that the job was done. Garret urgently wanted to open the door, to find out what was going on in there, to make sure Clarke was dead. Plus, with Alissa's help he'd be able to open the rest of the doors and find the boy.

So why couldn't he open the door?

Garret walked back to the room where Louis had been sleeping before his magnificent escape act. How did he get out? It made no sense to Garret, and it frustrated him to no end. Garret hated when things didn't make sense, he hated not knowing.

The bunk protested as Garret sat on it and rested his head in his hands.

'She's probably murdered the Captain by now.' He spoke aloud to no one in particular. It made him feel uneasy, calling her a murderer, but that was what she was now. Alissa was the child who murdered.

Garret walked back over to the bunker door and pressed the keys without even thinking about it. He needed to do it, he needed to free Alissa.

The doors slid open and started to reveal a gruesome story. Garret's heart sank as he looked at the entranceway. Alissa should've shot the captain here –

Garret saw her pull the gun as the door closed. But instead there was a chair on the floor, toppled onto its side with blood covering one leg. Garret started to feel sick when he saw the pool of blood beneath it. He could only hope it was the captain's.

'Alissa!'

Garret's call went unanswered but he clung to the vain hope that she would come running out to him. There was nothing but silence in the bunker. He shouted again, this time with more urgency, and again he heard no reply.

Garret continued through the bunker and everywhere he went he saw evidence of Alissa and the captain. The bed in the infirmary had been slept in, the captain's quarters had been used, but Alissa was nowhere to be found.

How did she get out and why had she taken the captain with her? Dead or alive, it made no sense to take him. Garret walked through the bunker looking for the escape route that Alissa had taken. His old eyes searched the walls, floor and ceiling in each room. Then he spotted it, the hatchway in the infirmary. Garret smiled to himself and climbed up onto the bed and pulled himself through the hole.

CHAPTER TWENTY-ONE

ALISSA NAMAAH AND CAPTAIN CLARKE ANDOVER walked silently through the long, grey corridors of New Amerland. Together they passed flashes of her old life, the canteen where Alissa feasted with her best friends, the bar they drank in when Saime's was shut; they even passed her little metal bench outside the box rooms. What would her father say if he saw her now?

Alissa was ready for this now and the captain followed behind her. They walked in silence as the awkwardness between them had come back. Clarke didn't know what was going to happen when they met the men in black suits, but he knew it wasn't going to be pretty. There was a good chance that Alissa would try to kill him to save her friend, and if that happened he didn't fancy his chances. On the other hand, he couldn't let his girl go into the lion's den alone.

Clarke's thoughts turned to his son. Louis was a smart boy, always thinking and keeping out of trouble, although these days he was quieter than usual. Ever since the accident. He might've escaped Garret and hopped the late night subways back to Swann Towers.

He would've been okay too, the subways were pretty deserted at that hour. Much like the rest of the complex.

'We're here.' Alissa spoke quietly but then she didn't need to raise her voice to get the captain's attention. Clarke looked at the door in front of them and his brow knitted slightly. He knew that behind it there was a short hall, barely more than a concrete passage that would lead to one of the open tunnels, one that the Unpleasant Ones regularly inhabited.

'Is this really the best way in?'

Alissa sighed as though frustrated at having to explain her decision to the Captain.

'It's the only way in. For us anyway. As part of my training I was given an intimate knowledge of this facility including all the secret areas that are used by the men. I can only assume they expected me to hide out there if there was a problem with the mission.'

'You mean if you'd been caught trying to murder me?' Clarke's voice had an edge to it. If they carried on down this route they'd end up arguing again and Alissa didn't have time for that. She looked Clarke dead in the eye. 'Yes. If I had been caught trying to murder you, I would've needed a place to escape to. Eventually I would've figured out that the only surveillance down here was theirs. Fortunately, I also know a way into the facility that they don't monitor.'

'Why don't they monitor it?'

The Captain's questions were becoming tedious for Alissa. 'They don't monitor it, Captain, because they don't need to. No person in their right mind is going to fight their way past the freaks in these tunnels just to get to a place they don't know exists.'

'You might.'

'And I suspect they realise that now and are currently trying to rectify this blind spot so we really do need to hurry. Sir.'

Clarke knew that the conversation was over as Alissa pulled a gun out of the left holster and opened the door. The filthy passageway smelled sour, like rancid food left in the bins behind the canteen. They reached the door at the other end of the corridor and Alissa turned to Clarke.

'I don't know what's going to happen in here, but I know that you're probably going to need this.' She held out the other gun. Clarke hadn't even seen her take it out of its holster. She was unquestionably good but the captain knew a thing or two about guns. He expertly flicked the arming switch and the gun let out a gentle hum. It was armed.

'I'm ready,' he said.
'Good.'

Alissa was still speaking softly as she pulled the door open and walked through into the tunnel, closely followed by the captain. They stood for a moment in silence, waiting for their eyes to adjust to the darkness; they were exposed and vulnerable without the full range of vision. Alissa took the knife out of her boot and held it tightly. A weapon in each hand made her feel safer – it was a comfort knowing she could defend herself against anything that came at her in this dank tunnel.

They were silently listening for any sounds, anything to make them think that something was out there, watching them. Everything was silent and still, so Alissa walked out into the middle of the tunnel, fully visible for anyone to see. If the Unpleasant Ones were going to attack, this would be the perfect time.

They had entered the tunnel from the side and needed to follow the path north for a few hundred yards. They walked without talking, both mentally preparing for any attack. Alissa held her gun in her right hand and her knife in the left.

The captain saw it first, since he was a few steps behind – a shadow to the side, moving silently. But before he could blink it had flown out and hit Alissa in the side. She was carried off her feet and hit the ground with a sickening thud. The captain had already started towards her, gun aimed at the shadow, ready to shoot, when he heard a noise behind him. He spun round and was face to face with a UO. It was less than a foot away, its mouth caked in what looked like blood.

The captain instinctively pulled the trigger and at point blank range the gun blew a hole in its chest. It flopped to the ground, and blood began to pool around as a gurgling sound came from its throat. But the captain was more concerned with the gun in his own hand. It had blackened round the barrel and was making an odd clicking sound.

Alissa was shocked by the force with which she was tackled. It knocked the breath right out of her, and as she hit the floor she had tears in her eyes and was fighting for air. She landed on her left side with the UO on top of her; shifted herself and tried to roll onto her back. As she did so she brought the handle of the knife into the side of the UO's face, knocking it off-balance. Alissa seized the opportunity to thrust the blade of her knife towards its head and the serrated blade slid into the temple of the UO with no resistance at all, Alissa's momentum carrying her arm until the hilt of the knife connected with the its skull.

Blood flowed freely as she pushed the creature from her and withdrew the knife.

Alissa climbed to her feet, sticky with the UO's blood and disgusted by how it felt on her hand. She spotted the captain a few feet away and smiled. He was safe. Then Alissa's ears picked up a frequency, something not right. A high-pitched whine was coming from the gun and it made her instantly sick to the stomach. Her feet barely touched the floor as she practically flew the distance between herself and Clarke.

His eyes were locked on the gun and the captain didn't even realise she was beside him. Alissa hit the back of his forearm with all her strength, knocking the gun out of his hand and causing it to land a few feet away; and as she grabbed his shirt and dragged Clarke away the pitch of the sound increased.

It got higher and higher, a warning to those with sufficient knowledge. Alissa pulled the captain to the ground before the gun exploded.

The shockwave was like nothing she had ever experienced. Her insides felt like they'd liquefied and her ears popped, causing massive pain throughout her head. It only lasted a few seconds but it was enough to leave her thoroughly shaken.

Alissa had dragged Clarke to the ground and curled into a protective ball around him. Her mind was whirling. The guns were sabotaged, but why? The weight of the gun still in her hand suddenly became more obvious. Alissa eyed it suspiciously.

'Are you okay?'

The captain's voice gave away the panic he felt. He looked at Alissa, who was holding the other gun and staring at it. 'He gave these to me.'

'Who did?'

'Silver Glove. I was supposed to use them to … kill you.'

Neither of them spoke after that. Silver Glove wanted her dead. That's the thought she was left with now. After she'd killed the captain the gun would've killed her too, cleaning up that loose end. If she'd shot the captain in the bunker they'd both be dead.

The gun fell from her hand as she relaxed her grip. She couldn't keep it now, it was a hindrance – if she took it into battle it could be used against her, or worse, by someone else to protect her. It was too dangerous to keep.

Alissa walked along, quietly reflecting on the last few minutes. The guns were a bust; all she had left was the knife so it would have to be enough. She slid it back into her boot, feeling the comforting pressure it put on her ankle. Her side was aching from the fall and the captain didn't look much better than she felt. They would get to the room soon enough and when they did she was going to end all of this once and for all.

The mission is what matters.

'Yeah, right,' she said quietly.

CHAPTER TWENTY-TWO

GARRET WAS CRAWLING ALONG THE AIR VENT THAT had previously been Alissa and the captain's escape route. He could see the scuff marks in the dust where they had crawled and knew he was going the right way.

The old man thought about what was going to happen now and he figured that Louis was going to raise the alarm – that much was obvious – then it would only be a matter of time before the police patrol units were hunting for him. And they would find him – they always found their man. One hundred percent success rate, the Board of Governors boasted.

After they caught him, they'd want him to confess all that he had done and they certainly wouldn't believe his story about the captain trying to destroy the Ark. After all, everything was based on what Alissa had told him and the disk from those men.

Those men. I've risked my life, career, everything – on something I heard from a stranger. His heart started pounding. Those men. He'd never even met them, didn't know their names. Would Alissa come forward and protect him? Probably not. He was in this alone now and he had to find the boy.

Garret was shaken out of his thoughts by his arrival at the end of the vent. The panel had been forced out and maintenance didn't come back on shift until the early hours of the morning. The drop was a long one for a man in his sixties but nevertheless he pushed himself to the edge and dropped down.

Garret recognised this place. If he got to the main city area then he could use a panel to locate Louis. He set off at a jog down the hallway.

***

The two new friends turned a corner and arrived at the main entranceway to the garages and maintenance hangars. Louis looked around and glared at the signs telling him where he was.

'This isn't where I live!' His voice was raised and his expression suddenly cruel. He turned to face Ham. 'Why have you brought me here?'

Ham looked at the young boy. 'I just need to run a quick errand before I took you home.'

'No!' Louis stamped his foot and his face contorted in anger. 'Take me to my quarters now!'

Ham stood over the little boy. 'If you want to go home you can, but I can't take you until I've done what I need to do.'

Ham turned and continued on towards the garages. Louis looked worried now. He bit his lip and watched Ham walk further away. He would have to follow the fat man, he had no choice.

***

This was it, the doorway to the end. Stop being so morbid, Alissa commanded herself. We could all survive this, escape Earth and live happily ever after. She glanced at the Captain. One of them was going to die in this room. All she knew for certain was that it couldn't be Shem. She had to save Shem. She swallowed the lump that was forming in her throat.

'Are you ready?' The Captain's voice was calm. *How is he not screaming at me? He must know! He must realise what's going to happen.* The thoughts spun through her head, barely making sense. The only words she could muster were, 'I'm ready.'

The captain pressed the buttons on the door and it slid open smoothly, revealing a terrible scene.

Alissa had expected them to be hidden deep in the centre of the facility – according to what she knew, there wasn't even a room here.

They've changed it. How could they do that? Change the interior of the building, move themselves wherever they wanted to go? Whatever technology they were using was far beyond anything a humble mechanic could grasp.

Alissa froze when she spotted Shem, tied to a white tiled wall, sweat covering his wonderful face and dripping onto his shirt. His feet barely touched the floor and he looked like he was in agony.

Alissa desperately fought the urge to run to him, to free him and hold him, to protect him and take him away, but focused instead on the mere fact that he was alive. She calmly crossed the threshold into the room, closely followed by the captain.

The four men turned their attention to their new guests and Alissa stood in silence as Silver Glove moved towards her; as he closed the gap his smile widened.

Vicious thoughts ran through Alissa's mind. She wanted to hurt him, tear him limb from limb, make him beg for mercy.

'Now now Alissa, that's not very nice.' His voice was dripping with condescension. He was her master.

'How did you ...' He couldn't hear her thoughts could he? That wasn't fair, how could she overcome that? How could she fight someone who knew her deepest secrets?

'Alissa, what's going on?' The captain sounded concerned but she ignored him. Silver Glove was all that mattered; he was invading her mind but she didn't want him to leave. The connection between them was tangible; after everything the men did to her, Silver Glove was there, encouraging her, promising ... Silver Glove was the one who helped Alissa to cope. Without him she would've died in the facility, she had neither the bravery nor the strength to succeed without him.

The door suddenly slid shut behind her.

Alissa flinched as their only exit was sealed off, but made no attempt to move. Her glazed eyes remained locked on Silver Glove as he smiled his wicked smile.

'What are you doing to her?' The captain's voice interrupted the violation of her mind. Her eyes focused on Silver Glove. He was smiling, and she was his again.

'Come now Alissa, you have work to do.' He wrapped his arm around her shoulder and guided her away from the captain, walking her over towards the centre of the room. Alissa didn't look back.

***

Ham walked to the room he and Alissa had been working in before all of this had happened. Back when everything was still okay and they were all going on the Ark together. The door slid open, revealing the enormous space filled with machinery. The garage itself was empty of people – no one would show up here until morning shift.

Ham walked in and bright lights came on overhead. Under the florescent glow he could see how filthy he really was. All the rolling around on the floor had taken its toll on his overalls and his outfit matched the walls a little too well in its familiar shade of grey.

Walking further into the room, Ham could hear the young boy's footsteps behind him. He knew the boy would follow and it was probably for the best; it would be all the proof he needed that his plan had worked.

He continued through the garage. He could see his destination. The boy started shouting at Ham to stop, begging him, screaming his name in a childish temper tantrum.

Ham ignored him. He wasn't about to be stopped by such a small specimen of life.

Crossing the room, Ham walked with purpose towards the machine he and Alissa had been working on. He still didn't understand it but he knew what needed to happen. He reached the alien technology and looked at it, he ran his fingers over the smooth panels, allowed himself to enjoy the feeling of the cool metal against his fingertips.

There were blue lights inside. They were beautiful, like no other shade of blue in the world. It was effervescent, luxurious and terrifying all at the same time. It was hopeless to describe it and impossible to forget.

He'd only seen a colour that vibrant once in his life and that was in the eyes of one of the men who took Shem. Ham was right about this; he knew it, but he also knew that his slow brain would not know how to break the secrets of this machine.

His fingers wrapped around the reassuring little packet in his pocket, the little packet that used to contain a green powder. His nose was still burning but he never made a sound, never missed a step when he took it. He didn't want the kid to know. The kid made this more complicated. Something about the little kid was wrong. No kid behaves that way.

***

'Remember why you're here Alissa. The captain wants everyone dead.'

Her gaze was dreamily locked on Silver Glove. Alissa fondly remembered her stay with him. He defended her, protected her from the wrath of the others. Silver Glove was the honest one among them. He taught her the truth about the captain.

The captain. He saved her life. In the bunker, he healed her face, told her about his son.

'His son.' Alissa's voice was barely a whisper.

'What?' Silver Glove only just heard the sound escape her lips.

'What about the captain's son?' said Alissa. She wanted to know the story from her truth-giver.

'What about him?'

'Why would the captain kill his own son? I saw him in the bunker; he was devastated about leaving his son.' Alissa turned slowly towards Clarke who stood alone, his back to the locked door. 'Why would you kill your own son?'

Silver Glove exhaled noisily, catching Alissa's attention once more. This is the moment I lose her.

'His son is dead.'

Alissa never took her eyes off the captain. She watched intently as his face crumpled into misery. His mouth opened but no sound came out. Tears streamed down his face. He was broken.

'How?' Her voice was small.

Silver Gloved glanced at his three companions and back to Alissa.

'His wife was assigned to the Hawk. An exploratory ship that was to map new mining routes just outside the solar system. It was agreed by my High Command that the mission would not take place and the ship's entire compliment of forty-seven people would be killed before they ever made it on board.'

He spoke to with such serenity, it would be easy to think he was talking about a tranquil holo-suite program and not the deaths of nearly fifty innocent people.

'You did it?' Alissa needed to know the rest.

'Sally Andover was taking her only son on a trip to Silver City. Their hovercar exploded en route and they were both killed instantly.

It was an attack orchestrated to look like an accident. No one would ever know what happened, and you can imagine our delight when we discovered that she was the wife of the latest captain to accept command of an Ark. We placed an agent in place of his son, to continue living as a normal child until activated.' Silver Glove turned to the captain. 'We destroyed your son's remains to hide the evidence of what had been done.'

Anger took hold of Clarke Andover and with tear-filled eyes he ran at Silver Glove; an animalistic scream came from his mouth. Three suited men came from nowhere and surrounded him in seconds, holding him against the white tile wall. Struggling and screaming, Clarke fought against them, frantically trying to free himself from their iron grip. Clarke Andover would not be stopped. He would kill them all. They took his son.

'Do you really believe that this will be your revenge, Captain?' Silver Glove was still smiling, still talking as if they were all friends talking casually about that they had done over the summer.

'I will kill you for this.' The captain's voice was vicious as he spat the words, filled with hate, at Silver Glove.

'No, Clarke. You are here, in my facility, restrained and weak. I got you here using the lovely, predictable Alissa.'

With that Silver Glove turned to face the girl who had stood quietly, listening to the mental torment that had been laid on the captain.

As Silver Glove's eyes met Alissa's, she bent slightly, slid the knife out of her boot and pointed it at Silver Glove's throat. He felt the sharp tip digging into his Adam's apple. His eyes revealed his betrayal.

'Tell me the truth. Why do you want Clarke to die?' Alissa surprised even herself with the steadiness of her voice.

'As you wish, my love.' Silver Glove stood there with the knife tip nudging at his throat with every word. Alissa stared into his eyes while he spoke. 'The truth is, we cannot let humans leave their own solar system. There are worse things out there than us and they don't want humanity scouring the galaxy colonising planets wherever they like. There is an order to space and you people are not ready for it. They will keep you here at all costs. They are the ones that controlled this mission.'

'Why the captain? Why kill him?' Her voice was rising.

'If a captain dies then the command of his ship is given to his second-in-command. Garret was in receipt of a file containing many things, including the destruction of the ship. A virus that will cause The Ark to critically malfunction'

'The disk ...' It was a stark realisation for Alissa. 'The disk destroys the ship. With the captain dead Garret is free to bring anything you plant on him onto that ship. After all, no one searches the captain. You just have to sit back and wait for Garrett to check the disk when he finds it.'

Alissa was horrified by the implications.

'You blew up all the other ships, didn't you!' Alissa screamed at him. The rage she felt at the suited man's confession was taking her over and she pressed the tip of the knife harder into his throat.

'Not this time. You've failed. I'm going to end this here and now. It's over.'

'What about Shem?'

It was like being punched in the face. What had she missed this time?

'What about him?' Her question was cautious, as if just asking it would cause Silver Glove to kill her best friend.

'Unless you kill Clarke Andover, Shem dies.'

Alissa looked over at her friend, hanging by his arms, unconscious and without a clue what was going on. Then her stare worked its way to the captain, still being held against the wall, waiting for her judgement. Alissa had to condemn one man to death, but which would it be?

Alissa lowered the weapon to her side and turned away from Silver Glove, her expression blank. She was defeated. The choice she had made broke her heart but she knew she had to do it.

With all of her newfound strength she spun around on the spot and raised her arm, swinging the knife towards Silver Glove, its razor-sharp edge glinting in the harsh glare of the lights as it arched like lightning through the air.

When Alissa's arm connected with Silver Glove's hand, for an instant she thought she had won. But then she felt his impossibly strong fingers close like a vice around her wrist. With his free hand he easily removed the knife from her grip and smiled his beautiful smile for her.

Alissa couldn't resist him. Even knowing everything about him, what he was and what he had done, she couldn't stop him. He placed his hand on the back of her neck and lowered his face towards her. His scent was intoxicating and it made her light-headed. Alissa Namaah loved him, with everything she had. Her eyes closed as she succumbed to his embrace.

Silver Glove couldn't think about this. She felt wonderful in his arms, so delicate and feminine. But she was weak. Alissa wasn't strong enough to complete her mission, but he would be. Silver Glove knew what was going to happen next and was glad, at least, that it would happen in his arms. He wanted to guide her through this, be with her for the rest of her life.

Silver Glove's arm drew back, and he thrust the knife deep into Alissa's abdomen. Her eyes flew open; she felt a dull throb where his hand had connected with her, but no real pain. She was in denial. Silver Glove hadn't done anything, and she was okay. It must've been an accident.

The truth was evident as she looked into his eyes. There was real agony there, staring her in the face. Alissa could hear someone shouting, but it wasn't her voice, or Silver Glove's. Was there someone else here? No, he did this. He's killed me.

Alissa's knees gave way and she collapsed in his arms. Silver Glove fell to the ground with Alissa and held her in his arms. 'Why?'

Her voice was a whisper. There was barely anything left.

'I'm sorry.'

***

Ham looked around the area and spotted his trusty laser saw. It was a perfect specimen of machinery, clean and in perfect working order. Ham took good care of his tools and never left them filthy or let anyone else use them. Some of the guys said he was weird about it but he didn't care.

Louis was still shouting his protest as Ham ran over and grabbed the saw. He sensed that it was only a matter of time before the kid attacked him, and he didn't really know how that would pan out. There was something wrong about the boy. Would he be stronger too?

Ham took the saw back to the machine and used it to gently cut one of the panels open; it fizzled as the hot metal melted under the red laser. Ham made a hole wide enough to lean into and look inside. The machine was intricate in its design and he understood now why Alissa had looked so perplexed when she was working on it. It wasn't human in its design and Ham realised that he had no idea how it was put together. The engine itself was emitting a low whirring noise and every surface reflected an eerie blue glow. 'Stop now, Ham.'

The voice was young but calm, and it caused Ham to freeze.

'I'd come out of there if I were you.'

Ham straightened slowly, horribly aware that his back was facing the child who caused his imagination to run riot. What would he see when he faced the kid? Ham wasn't sure he wanted to know.

'Turn around Ham.'

Ham slowly rotated and within seconds that could have lasted an eternity he was face to face with the voice.

Louis was staring at him with eyes wide and unblinking – unreal. Ham looked at the kid, so small and yet so determined, so frightening. Ham's gaze wandered from the boy's strange eyes down his arm, to the outstretched hand in which was held a gun. A gun aimed directly at Ham's chest.

No one had ever pointed a weapon at Ham before and all manner of thoughts began running through his head. None of them had a happy ending. He pictured the bullet ripping through his sternum and flying out of his back. Ham needed to think now; he needed to understand what he was facing. Would talking to Louis be the best idea?

'Put the gun down, Louis.' Ham was trying to be brave but the tone in his voice revealed his fear.

'I don't want to.'

'You don't understand what's happening here.'

'And you do? Tell me, Ham, how does someone like you figure out something like this? You're stupid and everyone knows it.' Louis' hand was steady as he pointed the gun. He walked towards the big man.

'You seem to think this is all so simple. Destroy the machine and you destroy the threat. But what if they're not the threat? What if you're the danger? Do you really know what will happen if you continue with your 'mission'?' Louis was now standing directly in front of Ham, looking up into his round face. 'Civilisations will fall at your hand.'

Ham's brain had only being paying attention to half of what Louis was saying. He was thinking, trying to work through the puzzle in front of him. All the clues were there and he just had to put it all together.

Louis was still staring hard at him, still pointing the weapon. Ham needed to step outside of this, look at it bit by bit. Dissect the scene unfolding before his eyes and discover what the secret was. His eyes travelled from the child's contorted face, to the machine by his side, then to the gun in Louis' hand.

Then Ham did something completely unexpected. He smiled. It all fell into place and he turned his back on Louis and leant back into the bowels of the machine.

'You know what Louis? I think you're right. I think that by destroying this thing I will save two very important people and that is worth dying for.' He reached his arms into the wiring and started feeling around. 'Don't you agree?'

'Get away from that!' Louis' voice was a screech.

'No.' Ham felt what he was looking for and tightened his grip on it. 'You hold in your hand a Mark Two Yankee Class Widow Maker. It's an impressive piece of machinery and I've seen pictures of them before. I'm actually a bit of a fan of weaponry. I also know that they stopped making that gun around one hundred years ago and the only two left in existence are locked away in an underground armoury that people like you and me will never see the inside of.'

'What are you saying?' The kid wasn't sounding so calm anymore.

'Your gun isn't real, Louis.'

With that Ham pulled his arm out of the machine, taking with it a good chunk of wiring and important-looking parts. Sparks flew out of the hole and showered Ham as he toppled backwards onto the metal flooring. He curled up to protect himself from the fiery flecks that burned as they landed on any exposed flesh.

Ham moved away from the machine and looked around the garage. Louis was gone. He knew that he'd been right all along and was pleased that he had done something right, for his friends, but he was exhausted now. The adrenaline had worked the enhancement drug out of his system faster than usual and it had left him completely drained.

He pushed himself along the floor and leant against the wall. He sat there, staring at the machine, tired but happy.

CHAPTER TWENTY-THREE

THE CAPTAIN FELL TO THE GROUND AS THE THREE men pinning him to the wall vanished without a sound. His palms took the brunt of the fall but his knees ached with the contact. A metallic clang told him the knife had fallen and when he raised his head, Clarke saw Alissa on the floor. The knife rested peacefully beside her, sticky with her blood, and Alissa was little more than a crumpled mess. Blood was seeping through her clothes and surrounding her in a crimson puddle. She wasn't breathing; he had destroyed her, the man in the silver glove.

Everything was moving slowly and Clarke was struggling to understand what was happening. The men were gone, he was safe, but the girl …

Clarke dived across the room to Alissa's side and put his hand on her wound. He had some knowledge of medical matters from his years as a captain – it was part of his basic training. As he pressed his palm against her wound the blood seeped through his fingers.

He'd seen too much of this girl's blood and now she was going to die. Right here on this dirty tile floor.

'ALISSA!' The voice screamed out from the other side of the room, causing Clarke to whip his head round. The man tied to the wall had come to and was screaming her name, over and over. Hopelessness and devastation were etched in his bloodied face. This man had clearly lost his love.

The captain, meanwhile, had had a sudden recollection, and he hoped it wasn't too late. Reaching into the side pocket of his combats he closed his hand around a cylinder and pulled out the spray. When he took his hand from the wound the blood began to flow again, which he took to be a good sign. Alissa's heart was still beating.

He sprayed the jagged opening, almost empting the can, and the blood slowed to a trickle. But the damage was already done. Clarke didn't know if she would survive this – he didn't know if anyone could survive this – but he had done all he could.

Standing up, he wiped his bloody hands on his shirt and crossed the room to the man tied to the wall. Shem's face was streaked with tears and sweat. The captain removed the pins from the shackles and Shem dropped to the floor.

Shem cried out as the tension was released from his arms; the pain in his shoulders was excruciating and his tear-streaked face was contorted in pain and emotion. He crawled to where Alissa lay and gathered her up into his aching arms. He sat with her, holding her, willing her to live.

The captain's voice was gentle as it interrupted him.

'Come on, we need to take her to the infirmary.'

Shem looked at her grimy face. She'd been through too much, and in the end he wasn't there to save her. If you get through this, Alissa, I will stay by your side forever. He would never let anything hurt her again.

Shem was going to be her protector, her best friend, and someday he would tell her the truth about his feelings.

Planning her future, visualising it, meant she wouldn't die and that's what he needed right now. Shem rose to his feet and lifted her carefully off the ground. He cradled her to his chest as he carried her out of the room.

Clarke Andover followed behind, allowing the tears of mourning for his son finally to fall freely down his face.

CHAPTER TWENTY-FOUR

THE NAVIGATION DECK ON BOARD THE ARK WAS A vast room filled with hundreds of officers inputting co-ordinates and making calculations to ensure the ship stayed on course. The Ark was such an enormous piece of machinery that it took constant adjustment just to prevent one edge trying to fly faster than the other.

The area was split into sections and each section had its own team of officers, and a chief. Shem's team were all working hard, their hands flying over the keypads in front of them, entering the required information to keep their boat afloat.

Their chief navigating officer sat behind his desk, facing the team but looking at no one in particular. His eyes had glazed over for the hundredth time that day, indicating that his thoughts were not currently with the ship. His team noticed, of course, but there was a deep respect for superiors within the ranks of the crews and they knew better than to pry into his personal business.

The story of the captain's attempted assassination had spread throughout the complex like wildfire and virtually the entire crew knew why Shem's arm was securely cradled in a sling. Being hung from the wrists had pulled his left arm almost out of the socket, which made his carrying of Alissa even more impressive.

Most people on board thought some of the stories were exaggerated, but Shem knew the truth of that night, and the horror. No matter how hard he tried, he couldn't free his mind from the image of Alissa dying on that tiled floor, bleeding out, her light fading. Shem blinked hard and tried to focus on the numbers in front of him, distracting himself from the fact that Alissa was still in the Ark's infirmary.

The captain had insisted on her transfer from New Amerland to the ship – said they couldn't fly without their Chief of Security – and now Dr Harper was tending to Shem's best friend, keeping her alive as best she could.

Ham and Shem had kept a vigil outside the medi-bay, refusing to leave until Alissa was awake. They hoped that somehow she knew they were there, waiting for her.

A loud chime startled Shem, bringing him into the present and drawing his attention to his personal terminal. He pulled the device out of his pocket and flicked a switch on the side. The call was from the captain.

'Chief, I have some news.'

Clarke's face wasn't giving anything away but Shem studied it anyway, desperate for some clue as to Alissa's condition. The captain continued. 'I've just had word from Dr Harper. Alissa's awake.'

Shem dropped the control pad and jumped up from his seat. His team knew he was preoccupied day and night, and allowances were being made. The nav deck doors flew open as Shem went through them, taking corners on the run and covering the journey along brightly lit corridors at full speed.

The Ark was much more beautiful than the complex he was used to. The corridors were cream and lined with thick carpet, something most people never got to see. The lights overhead were slightly warm in colour, nothing like the fluorescents that Shem had grown used to over the years. Everything was softer here, more gentle, infinitely more comfortable.

Shem took the last corner before the infirmary at a jog, and arrived just in time to see Ham catching his breath outside, with Garret resting one hand on his shoulder. Clarke came out of the infirmary and smiled at the mix of people standing awkwardly together.

The air was thick with excitement and anticipation. Alissa was important to all of them now. She had touched each of their lives and they all appreciated that in different ways. The four men walked into the infirmary and turned towards the medi-bay.

It was dimmer in her room, more quiet – engine noise and the whirr of machinery were oddly absent, making the room feel like it was in the complex. It was subtly decorated in neutral tones – healing tones, thought Shem – and the walls were hung with framed landscapes from before the Incident. Shem thought that if he was unconscious, then this was the place he would like to wake up in. There were even fresh flowers on the cabinet beside Alissa's bed.

Alissa's eyes were open and she was looking around, confusion etched on her face.

'We're in space?'

She sounded croaky when she spoke; she hadn't used her voice in a week. The four men looked at each other and silently asked each other how she knew …

Shem walked across the room and sat beside her on the bed; he took her hand in his and squeezed it reassuringly.

'We launched two days ago. How did you know?'

'I'm a mechanic, Shem. I can tell when a boat is sailing.' She made an attempt at a weak smile before a realisation hit her. 'Are we safe?

What happened?' She tried to sit up, to get out of bed.

If Silver Glove had got away, she would find him.

'We're safe, Alissa.' The captain walked towards her as Shem gently but firmly prevented her from leaping out of the bed. 'Ham figured it out in the end.' As he spoke, Ham stood behind him, nodding vigorously. 'The four men were holograms, Alissa. Like the ones in the suites. You can touch them, smell them. You'd have no way of knowing they weren't real.'

Alissa's head dropped a little, her eyes half-closing as she thought about the way Silver Glove had smelled. It was intoxicating, and even now her heart ached for him to come back. He'd done something to her, made her his own – ruined her.

'They were projected by the alien machine the two of you were working on,' the captain continued. 'We still don't know exactly where the signal was coming from. But it was way outside of our solar system.'

'What about your son?'

Alissa's question hit the captain hard. The pain on his face was obvious and she regretted her words immediately. Why hadn't she just waited? She could've asked Shem or Ham later.

'Louis died a long time ago, and from what I can tell the hologram I was living with thought he was my son right up until Garret locked him away. That's when they activated him and he became their agent.'

'I'm sorry.' She meant it. The captain turned away and walked towards the window, indicating that his part in this conversation was over.

Alissa looked at Garret. 'So how did I end up here? I failed the aptitude test. There isn't a place for me.'

Garret was smiling. 'The ship couldn't leave without its Chief of Security.'

So there she was, lying in a bed, surrounded by people who cared about her. She had made it off planet Earth and was ready for a new life on the Ark. They would find a new world and send the message back and more people would follow. They would save the world.

The story continues in

T H E

PRISON

J   S W I F T

ACKNOWLEDGEMENTS

This story could not have happened without the help of the following people.

Ken Dalrymple, for your constant support.
Paul Cringle, for the epic chapter images.
BNBS, for showing me how it's done.
Miblart, for the amazing cover art.
Mike Faulkner, for being a brilliant copy editor.

ABOUT THE AUTHOR

Jennifer Swift has been an avid science fiction fan for many years. Surrounding herself with books and TV shows that captured her imagination. From Star Trek to Red Dwarf, the idea of space travel has implanted itself deep within her mind, inspiring a series that not only stays true to science fiction, but offers an array of likeable and realistic characters that you can't help but become attached to.

Printed in Great Britain
by Amazon

86191286R00125